SUBMISSION

A Treasury of Women
Who Like to Give In
A Mischief Collection of Erotica

T0337292

mischief

Mischief
An imprint of HarperCollins*Publishers*
77–85 Fulham Palace Road,
Hammersmith, London W6 8JB

www.mischiefbooks.com

A Paperback Original 2013

First published in Great Britain in ebook format by
HarperCollins*Publishers* 2012

A catalogue record for this book is
available from the British Library

ISBN-13: 9780007534814

Set in Sabon by FMG using Atomik ePublisher from Easypress

Find out more about HarperCollins and the environment at
www.harpercollins.co.uk/green

Contents

Contents

Best in Show
Rose de Fer

I fidget, fussing with the hem of my dress as the car glides to a stop before an imposing Victorian house. The driver opens my door and I glance nervously up at him. He hasn't said a word throughout the drive and I can make out no expression behind his mirrored sunglasses. He merely waits for me to get out. I take a deep breath and step down on to the gravel. It's the last time I'll be allowed to walk upright for a while and I can't fight the powerful fear that threatens to make my legs buckle. The driver returns to the car and immediately pulls away, disappearing down the long winding drive. I am alone.

Slowly I make my way to the porch where a folded note bearing my name – Saskia – lies on the doormat. With trembling fingers I fumble it open.

'Undress,' it says. 'Scratch on the door when you are ready.'

I glance behind me. Fields and woodland stretch away into the chilly mist, but there is no one around, no one to watch as a frightened young woman strips naked outside a stately home. I'm not the first either. A small basket contains various items of clothing. Two pairs of shoes – sexy red stilettos and silver ballet flats – stand neatly to one side.

I know I mustn't delay so I quickly slip out of my dress, fold it neatly and add it to the basket. I unlace my strappy black sandals and place them next to the ballet flats. The tiled porch chills my bare feet. I hesitate only a moment before unhooking my bra and peeling my knickers off. I drop my lacy underthings into the basket and, stomach fluttering, I sink to my knees on the rough hessian doormat. I close my eyes, count to three and scratch gently at the large oak door.

Soon I hear the sharp taps of approaching footsteps. My heart gives a startled leap as the door opens and I look up into the face of a stranger. The man is immaculately dressed in a soft grey suit and shiny black shoes. He has a kind, handsome face and he smiles at me as he reaches down to ruffle my hair.

'Good girl,' he says, holding the door open. 'Come on, in you come.'

I creep inside on all fours, peering around curiously at

the unfamiliar surroundings. The hallway is opulent and elegant. A high stained-glass window casts its image on the marble floor, staining my hands with reflected colours.

I hear the door close and then the man is crouching in front of me. He holds a thin strip of red leather in his hands and I realise he must be the handler. I obediently lift my head so he can fasten the collar around my neck. There is the soft jingle of a metal tag and I feel its chill against my throat. The collar is a strange comfort. It crystallises my position more than any other single step in the elaborate ritual. It instantly suffuses me with warmth and security, inducing a powerful feeling of submission.

As the man clips a lead to my collar I lower my head. He gives the lead a gentle tug and I follow him down the corridor and into a room towards the back of the house. The low murmur of male voices grows louder as we approach. I hesitate in the doorway, peering in.

We've come to what looks like a ballroom, although the room is obviously not used for dancing. The floor is covered with thick, luxurious Oriental rugs that cushion my knees as I am led inside. A huge space has been cleared in the middle, bounded by a semicircle of chairs. A show ring. Some of the men are seated and several others stand off to one side, talking amongst themselves. A fire roars warmly in the hearth along the near wall and two women, naked like me, kneel before it.

'Saskia.'

I look up in response to the familiar and cherished voice of my master and I find myself quivering with happiness as he emerges from the group and comes towards me. I kneel up to reach him, placing my palms against his legs as he strokes my face tenderly.

'Who's a good girl?' he says. 'Is my little pet going to make me proud today?'

I nod my head, pawing gently at him with one hand. He smiles indulgently at my puppyish behaviour before unclipping my lead. Then he reaches into his pocket to withdraw a morsel of chocolate. I nibble the treat from his hand while he scratches me roughly behind the ears. If I had a tail I would wag it.

He points towards the fireplace then and tells me to join the others. I leave his side reluctantly and make my way across the plush carpet to where the other two women kneel, watching me.

One is a lithe golden blonde with cropped hair and full breasts. She looks to be in her mid-thirties, like me. She offers me a sunny smile and I shyly return it. The tag on her collar says PHOEBE. The other girl seems extremely self-conscious, although I can't see why. She's the prettiest of us, with long black hair, olive skin and striking blue eyes. A petite, almost boyish figure. She looks away as I take my place with them by the fire.

'It's Tara's first time,' I hear a man say, presumably her master.

It's my first time too and I can't believe anyone could be more nervous than I am. Phoebe nudges closer to me and places her hand on mine, her eyes shining with friendly encouragement. She seems to contain an immense amount of energy; she's practically buzzing with suppressed eagerness.

'Shall we start with Phoebe, then?'

She perks up at the deep voice, abandoning me in favour of her master, who pats his leg and calls to her. She bounds over to him and adopts a puppy play-bow, arms flat on the ground, back arched, bottom high in the air. Then she barks and leaps up, playfully grabs the lead in her teeth and scampers back to the fireplace with it. There isn't a trace of self-consciousness in her. She fully inhabits her role with gleeful abandon.

The watchers seem charmed by her antics, chuckling good-naturedly as her master feigns exasperation and goes to fetch her. She drops the lead when he tells her to and blinks up at him, wide-eyed and adoring, as he fastens it to her collar and walks her over to the handler and passes him the lead.

'She's all yours, Mr Veith.'

The handler gives Phoebe an affectionate pat on the head and the show begins. He takes her through a series of basic obedience commands – sit, stay, fetch – and then leads her around the ring. She is very nimble on all fours, much more so than I am, and she tosses her head as she

5

prances past the men I take to be the judges. Her enthusiasm is infectious and I find myself looking forward to my turn in the ring, my turn to show how good I can be, how obedient and responsive.

The judges mark their cards, occasionally smiling at something Phoebe does, occasionally frowning in serious contemplation. From time to time the handler rewards her with a treat – a small biscuit shaped like a bone. I worry at first that it's a genuine doggy biscuit. Phoebe is so lost in the role it wouldn't surprise me if she didn't notice. But when he tosses one near us and commands her to fetch it, I catch the smell of gingerbread and smile.

There is a small round of applause at the end of the performance and Phoebe dances in place, made even friskier by all the attention. Mr Veith lets her off the lead and tells her to stay and, although she clearly doesn't want to sit still, she obeys. Then she watches with keen interest as her master places a low grooming table in the centre of the room. Mr Veith joins him and Phoebe seems not the slightest bit nervous or uncertain as the two men lift her up and set her on all fours on top of it.

Her master stands in front of her and nods to the handler. 'She's ready.'

Mr Veith removes his jacket and rolls up his sleeves. Phoebe looks round at him as he approaches but her master gently guides her head back so that she is facing him instead. Mr Veith studies the naked woman before him, running his hands over her body as though testing the firmness of her skin. He squeezes her breasts one at a time and then pushes her lower back down, arching her body to raise her bottom up. She parts her thighs without being told and I see the men share a grin. It's obvious they know her well.

Mr Veith slowly draws a finger over the curve of each cheek, making her shudder. Then he slips his hand between her legs. She closes her eyes and a sigh of pleasure escapes her lips as she abandons all her canine mannerisms. Throughout the examination Phoebe never once seems embarrassed or discomfited. My heart begins to pound as I realise that I am likely to be subjected to the same intimate inspection and I know there is no way I'll have the composure that she does. Beside me Tara gives a soft little whimper and I take some perverse comfort in knowing that at least I'll handle it better than she will. I hope so anyway.

I glance over at my master, who is watching with detached interest. I lift my head, trying to catch his eye, but he studiously avoids my pleading gaze. Chastened by his silence, I turn back to the tableau in the centre of the room. Phoebe's master is holding her firmly by the arms now, keeping her still. Mr Veith's hand is well out of sight between her legs and Phoebe moans and gasps without a trace of shame. Suddenly I envy her fiercely, wishing I could be as uninhibited – as both a pet *and* a person.

Whatever he's doing to her soon proves too much and she reaches a fast and noisy climax. Blushing, I turn away, although I know she can't mind my watching. The room is filled with spectators, after all. I'm sure she relishes the attention.

Her master praises her and Mr Veith smilingly says she has done very well. The judges sombrely mark their cards, although I can't imagine what criteria they're evaluating.

The two men help Phoebe down and she makes her way over to me on all fours, wobbling slightly. Her face is flushed and glowing as she offers me a lopsided grin. She looks positively radiant. I bite my lip, too flustered to return her smile fully. I wonder if my arousal is as obvious to her as hers was to me?

Tara cowers on my other side, head down. I can sense her unease, although my intuition tells me it's only the public display that she objects to. I suspect I am the least experienced of the three of us.

The judges confer quietly and I silently hope I will be next. I'm so nervous about the prospect I'm lightheaded but I know that I absolutely don't want to be last. Better to dive in at the deep end and get it over with than linger on in torturous suspense.

'Let's have Tara next,' says Mr Veith.

My heart sinks.

Tara cringes and backs away towards the fire. For a

moment I worry she'll burn herself but then her master comes forward. He's young. Early twenties, I guess, probably the same age as his pet. He doesn't convey the authority of either my master or Phoebe's.

'Tara, come,' he says sharply. He snaps the lead to her collar and pulls her like a reluctant mule into the centre of the room. 'She hasn't really been trained yet,' he mumbles.

'Well, let's take her around the ring at least,' says the handler, holding his hand out for the lead.

But Tara refuses to move. Mr Veith tugs at the lead, first gently and then more firmly. He tries coaxing her with a biscuit but she turns her head away. I glance over at her master, who slouches at the edge of the ring, hands shoved deep into his pockets, frowning at the floor. The judges' pens scratch away in the background.

'Oh dear,' says Mr Veith. 'Quite a stubborn streak.'

'You have no idea.'

'Shall we just proceed to the examination?'

Her master shrugs.

Tara struggles as she is lifted on to the table. Her master tells her to be still and when she doesn't obey he flicks the end of the lead smartly against her backside, making her yelp.

I edge closer to Phoebe, who presses against me with silent reassurance. She nuzzles my face and I return the affectionate gesture. She's back in full puppy mode and for one crazy moment I'm tempted to pounce on her and instigate a game of play-fighting. But I don't dare. Not until my turn has passed.

We look back to see Tara's master holding the lead firmly while the handler strokes her and tries to calm her. The black waterfall of hair hides her eyes and Mr Veith gathers it in one hand and draws it aside to peer into her face. She stubbornly turns her head away and he tightens his grip on her hair to hold her still. Her eyes blaze with defiance. Across the room several of the men shift and murmur to one another. There is more scratching of pens.

'Spirited,' Mr Veith says, although I can't tell whether his tone is admiring or disapproving.

When he reaches out to touch Tara again she bares her teeth at him and he frowns. Her master says her name in a warning tone and she closes her lips, only slightly cowed. Mr Veith tries again to approach her and this time she snaps at him. I jump as I hear her teeth clack together in the air just beyond his fingers.

'Bad girl!' her master says, his voice low and harsh.

Tara glares at both men and shakes her hair free of the handler's grasp.

'I'm very sorry,' Mr Veith says, 'but I'm going to have to disqualify her.'

Her master scowls and Tara lowers her head like a puppy scolded for biting the postman. He gathers her up and sets her on the floor, her body language conveying both ongoing rebellion and regret at having disappointed her master. In my submissive state the scene distresses me intensely and I watch in horror as he leads her to a cage in the corner of the room and shoos her inside. He latches it closed and shakes his finger at her. 'Bad girl,' he says again. Then, shaking his head, he returns to his seat and flops into it with a heavy sigh.

Beside me Phoebe grins and I immediately feel silly. Of course. For Tara, this is what it's all about. Indeed, now that she's safe in her cage I see the corners of her mouth curl in a mischievous smirk. As far as she's concerned, she's won. I know at once that the red stilettos outside are hers.

Mr Veith sighs and addresses my master. 'Well, looks like it's Saskia's turn.'

My stomach plunges with fear. Although nothing but simple obedience is expected of me, I still feel unprepared. I know I can't compete with Phoebe. I also know I'll have to be extra good following Tara's outburst. Suddenly the pressure seems overwhelming. I whimper and press myself close to Phoebe, who gives my hand a friendly squeeze.

'Come along, Saskia,' my master says, smiling indulgently, 'there's a good girl.' He holds out one of my chocolate treats and I nibble it gratefully from his hand, my submission enhanced by the fact that everyone is

11

watching me. He delivers me to the handler and I peer up at him, telling him with my eyes what a good little doggy I'll be for him. I lift one hand slightly and Mr Veith smiles, bending down to shake it. He strokes my head and then we're off.

He leads me around the ring at a slower pace than Phoebe and I keep to his heel as I'm supposed to. I stop when he stops, turn when he turns and sit when I'm told to. He takes out one of his bone-shaped biscuits and holds it high over my head. I gaze up at it, knowing I mustn't jump up and snatch it, however much I want to.

'Good girl,' he says at last, lowering the biscuit so I can have it. I was right; it's gingerbread.

When I look over at the judges I see smiles on more than one face as they write. I don't need to see my master to know I've done well.

Mr Veith takes me around the ring one final time and, while I'm not the exhibitionist Phoebe is, I sense that I'm putting on a good show. It's over far too quickly and when I remember what comes next I start getting anxious. I try to hide my fear as Mr Veith leads me to the table and my master helps him lift me up on to it. He unclips the lead and I lift my head, happy not to need restraining like Tara. I am determined to make my master proud.

Mr Veith pats my head and I smile shyly, reassured

by the silent praise. I jump when I first feel his hand on my naked back, but he strokes me gently and I soon relax into his unfamiliar touch. His hands explore every inch of exposed flesh, running along my back and up and down my arms and legs. He lifts my feet and strokes them, then peers at my hands. He takes his time with me, no doubt feeling somewhat cheated by Tara.

I flinch, ticklish, as he draws his fingers along my ribs. Then he deftly slides his hands underneath me, cupping my small breasts. A hot pulse surges through my body and I feel myself growing wet as he squeezes me gently. Then he releases me and I feel a hand at the base of my spine, pushing down.

'Sit,' he instructs.

I sink to my knees and he moves in front of me and positions me how he wants me: kneeling up, back arched, arms at my sides. I lower my eyes demurely as he palms my breasts again, this time brushing his thumbs slowly back and forth over the nipples. They respond immediately and I push aside my self-consciousness, giving in to the stimulation. He lingers, his continued touch a reward for my good behaviour. I moan softly when at last he stops and I hear my master chuckle softly.

'Good girl,' he whispers, appearing at my side and feeding me another bite of chocolate. The heavenly taste fills my mouth, a perfect counterpoint to the tingling in my body, the hot pulsing in my sex.

Now Mr Veith urges me back up on all fours again. I obey instantly, eager to please, keen for more. His right hand glides up the inside of my left thigh and I hold my breath as I wait for the touch I'm craving. I sense that nothing less than full surrender will satisfy my master and I'm determined not to let my inhibitions get the best of me. I want what Phoebe had.

He pats the inside of each thigh, urging my legs apart. I gasp as the exposure chills the dampness that must be obvious to him. With one finger he explores the delicate folds, as though coaxing open the petals of a flower. He traces the opening of my sex, teasing me beyond endurance. I can't restrain a little moan of desire and my hips writhe, pleading, demanding.

'Very good,' he says, although whether he means my physical response or my general submission I have no idea. But he doesn't give me much time to wonder before he finally slips a finger inside me. The sensation is electric after the painful wanting and I clench tightly around his finger. He reaches deep inside, sweeping around the soft walls and nudging against my cervix. It makes me gasp. My legs tremble with the effort of not collapsing and he steadies me with his left hand.

I steal a glance over at Phoebe and she looks as rapt as I'm sure I did when it was her turn. She catches me looking and gives me a lascivious wink. The thought steals into my mind that the two of us could get up to some fun games on our own – assuming our masters would allow it, of course.

Mr Veith slides his finger out and I protest with a whimper before realising it's only so he can insert a second one. The penetration becomes rougher as he stretches me wide, manipulating me with clear expertise. At the same time he presses against my abdomen from the outside, as though trying to make his fingers meet on either side of my skin. I feel gorgeously invaded from every angle. I can't escape and I don't want to. Some part of me is vaguely aware of the rude display I'm making, grinding my hips wantonly as I am fondled before a room full of strangers. But I don't care. All I want is more. Too much could never be enough.

The signs must be obvious to him because suddenly he directs all his attention to my sex, slipping his left hand down to tweak the tiny little bud that will make me lose control. Almost immediately I feel the rising tide of a powerful climax and it overtakes me like a wave, crashing over me and pulling me under. I cry out, lost somewhere between pleasure and pain.

Starbursts blink behind my eyes and the only sound is my breathing as I pant and gasp for air. From far away I hear words of praise but I'm adrift in a world of ecstasy and can't make them out. Warm arms encircle me and I am lifted and then lowered to the floor, where it takes me a little while to remember how to make my arms and legs work. When I return to the fireplace I curl into a contented little ball, basking. Phoebe nuzzles me and kisses my cheek and I paw at her.

'Well, gentlemen,' comes the voice of Mr Veith some time later, 'it would appear we have a tie.'

Phoebe and I share a smile at the murmurs of approval from the crowd. He calls us both to the centre of the ring and we go eagerly, sitting side by side at his feet. He gives each of us a treat and addresses the room.

'I propose to add a new round to the competition. We've seen how the competitors interact with a handler. Now let's see how they interact with each other.'

I see Phoebe's eyes flash with mischief but before she can act, I do what I've been wanting to do all day: I pounce on her, knocking her flat on her back. She yelps in surprise but quickly recovers, rolling on to her front and preparing for the counterattack. I retreat a few steps and she launches herself at me, pinning me down and licking my face. I struggle beneath her, not with any real effort, and she eventually lets me up so we can trade places.

As we tussle my imagination goes wild and I fantasise that we're outside in the garden, frolicking in the grass, in the sprinkler, in the mud, getting filthy. We wouldn't be allowed back in the house then. Not without a bath. I can see us sitting together in a big metal tub on the patio, splashing in the soapsuds and the spray from the garden hose before being roughly towelled dry by our masters.

Someone tosses a foam toy into the ring and I grab it first, scampering away with Phoebe in hot pursuit. When she catches me she wrestles me to the floor and we tug it back and forth with our teeth, quickly reducing it to a scattering of fluff. I have never felt so free. By the time I finally capitulate and let her win, it's no longer about the game. Or the show.

I'm too exhausted to resist when Phoebe finally pushes me down, breathing hard from more than just the physical exertion. She fixes me with her beautiful gaze and caresses my face, drawing her hands lightly down my throat and over my breasts. I tremble and urge her on with a look. She hesitates only a moment before obliging. My sex is begging for her touch.

Phoebe strokes my silky wetness and bends down, covering my mouth with hers. Her kisses taste like ginger. As we surrender to our mutual attraction, I hear her tag jingle against her collar like a bell.

I arch my back and see my master standing nearby, watching us, smiling. I know I've made him proud even though I didn't win. But I imagine he has some more rigorous training in mind for his little pet. At least I hope so. For now I'm more than happy to let the winner have the spoils.

The Usual Dress Code
Elizabeth Coldwell

The e-mail arrives in her inbox without warning. 'Meet me at the Windsor Club for lunch tomorrow. One o'clock sharp. Be sure to observe the usual dress code.'

Even that simple message is enough to have her juices flowing as she reads and rereads it. So the lecture tour's over and he's back in the country, is he? So like him, she thinks, to arrive with no prior notice and expect her to fall back into their usual routine. But he knows she'll be there. She doesn't have plans for tomorrow lunchtime and, even if she did, she'd cancel them to be with him.

Though the work is stacked high on her desk, data needing to be inputted from a pile of forms, it's hard to concentrate on anything now she knows she's going to be seeing him again. Thoughts of him, and what he'll require her to do, push everything else to the back of her mind.

'The usual dress code.' Those four words contain the essential truth of their relationship: that he gives the orders and she willingly obeys them. From the day they met, he recognised the submissive heart of her, the part she'd never revealed to anyone for fear of being misunderstood. Even now, she still dreads the reaction from some friends and colleagues if they were ever to find out about the things he makes her do. To them, submissive means weak, easily trampled on, a personality lost and submerged beneath another's. She knows the truth: submitting makes her stronger, allows her to explore desires that would otherwise go unfulfilled. And the rules of the game are simple. If she says 'stop', they stop.

He'll love the outfit she bought in his absence, she thinks, giving up any pretence of work for the afternoon. His dress code is weirdly specific. If pressed, she'd define it as 'slutty 1950s secretary', fantasy fodder for the older, highly educated gentleman. Underwear that nips in her waist and thrusts out her breasts, giving her an exaggerated hourglass figure she suspects no real woman has ever possessed. Tight pencil skirts that give a wiggle to her walk, blouses with a fussy pussy bow at the neck, and gorgeous but impractical stockings. He likes them so sheer as to be practically invisible, with a fully fashioned heel and a seam running arrow-straight up the back of her legs. The straightness of the seam is very important – she's learned that over the years – and leaving them crooked is the quickest way to earn a couple of hard swats to her barely clad backside. If feminine intuition isn't a myth, it must have compelled her to spend time browsing her favourite vintage lingerie site, snapping up a couple of pairs of stockings in her size in preparation for his return. The parcel sits in her top desk drawer, delivered to her this morning by the office post-boy, who doesn't have a clue about her secret life but would probably nurse his erection for the rest of the day if he knew she was planning to truss herself up in seamed nylons and a six-strap suspender belt for the delight of a man who loves to see her wearing nothing else.

Every minute will drag till she's in his company once more. Her pussy is already wet and swollen with need but, from the time she receives his written instructions to the time she meets him, playing with herself is forbidden. He's very insistent about that. Once, he made her wait from Monday till Friday, four whole days spent stewing with frustration so acute she could barely stand it. She'd never be able to properly explain why she obeys him to the letter in this regard. All she can say is that if she disobeyed him, he'd know. He always knows.

The Windsor Club belongs to a bygone world. It is set on a quiet side street just off Piccadilly, a place where men can eat and doze and chat, away from any kind of female influence. Although the staff who fetch drinks on silver salvers and serve generous portions of nursery food at tables covered with crisp white cloths are all pretty young waitresses, she can't help but notice.

Arriving a couple of minutes before one, she announces herself at the front desk. The black-jacketed flunky looks her up and down, regarding her from tight blonde chignon to dizzying four-inch heels. Clearly not the usual choice of dining companion for the club's members, but he responds with a polite 'Ah, yes, Miss Culver. Professor Matlow is expecting you. Please come through.'

The club's main room is almost soporific in its warmth, after the February chill of the West End. He's sitting in a wing-backed leather armchair, reading this morning's copy of *The Times*. All she can see is the top of his head, dark curls shot through with more grey than she remembers, and his long legs in faded olive corduroys, crossed at the ankles. Just that glimpse causes her heart to lurch and a thin trickle of juice to seep into her black silk French knickers.

Robert Matlow, professor of English at one of the country's most respected universities and a world-renowned authority on the work of John Donne. Not that she ever addresses him by his given name. To her, he is never anything other than 'Sir'.

Hearing her approach, he folds his paper and lays it

on the table in front of him, next to the inevitable glass of twelve-year-old single malt. She wonders whether his instructions to the waitress as to how it should be served are as precise as the ones he always gives her. Two ice cubes. No more, no less. He requires his whisky to be chilled, not watered down. Nothing should impair its subtle, peaty taste, as he so often tells her. Perhaps one day he'll realise she's sometimes careless with the number of cubes simply to earn herself an extra stroke on her final punishment. Perhaps he already knows, and indulges her. Though she doubts that. From her experience, he is very seldom indulgent.

'Matilda. Punctual as ever, I see.' For the second time in a minute, she is scrutinised from head to toe. Where the door flunky looked at her with politely concealed lechery, this is a very different kind of inspection. His deep-set blue eyes check that she has, as he requested, observed the dress code – at least as far as he can tell from the outer layers of her clothing. They seek out any imperfections in her appearance: smudged lipstick; a stain on the sleeve of her cream jacket; a slight deviation in the straight lines of her stocking seams. He appears almost disappointed to find none.

'Do sit down,' he urges her, before beckoning the waitress over. 'Could you fetch the young lady a glass of white Burgundy?'

'Certainly, sir.'

And so it begins. He hasn't asked her what she might like, and by taking the choice away from her he has subtly reinforced his dominance within their relationship. She can't explain quite why this show of control turns her on so much; all she knows is that it's suddenly hard to focus on anything but the pulse beating insistently in her pussy.

'So, how are you, Matilda?'

With those words, he gives her permission to enter into conversation. He could just as easily have returned to his perusal of the obituaries, making her wait till he was ready to speak to her, but even though he'd never admit it to her face, she knows he's missed their regular chats.

'I'm fine, thank you, sir. Work's as boring as ever. How was America?'

The waitress returns and places a glass in front of her. He motions with his eyes for her to take a sip. She does, savouring the complex, buttery taste of the wine. It's an excellent choice, but she wouldn't have expected anything less. He's taught her so much in the time they've been together, not only in the bedroom. Before him, she existed on microwaved ready meals and supermarket plonk and never read anything more challenging than the weekly gossip magazines. He has refined her palate, given her a thirst to learn more about the world and fill the many gaps in her education.

He grins, the lines around his eyes deepening, one of the few reminders that he's almost fifteen years older than her. With his boundless vitality and body he keeps honed with an exercise regime bordering on the obsessive, it's sometimes hard to believe they aren't the same age. 'Oh, it's always nice to have a new audience for my one-liners.'

At his urging, she once sat in on one of his lectures, hidden away at the back of the darkened theatre. His dissection of love metaphors in metaphysical poetry went completely over her head, though some poem of Donne's in which he complained about how long it took for his lover to undress for bed still stuck in her mind, thanks to the outrageous manner in which he had acted it out, a neat pantomime of impatient male and coy female. He had the knack of keeping his students hanging on every word, enthralled by his obvious personal magnetism and unfettered sexuality. She'd overheard a couple of girls talking on the way out, describing all the deliciously filthy things they'd like to do to Professor Matlow if they got him alone. If only you knew, she thought.

Taking a sip of his whisky, he continues, 'Seriously, it was very productive. I've made some useful academic contacts, and one of the senior editors at the Harvard University Press is very keen to read the manuscript of my Donne biography, but four months on your own in hotel bedrooms grows a little wearying by the end.'

She's about to ask him more, happy to bask in the reflected glow of his success, but they're interrupted by the arrival of a man she doesn't recognise. He's around her own age, and it wouldn't surprise her if he was another academic; he has the same dishevelled dress sense and distracted air, as though he's not properly connected to the world around him. He pushes a stray lock of blond hair out of his eyes, before thrusting out his hand.

'Robert, great to see you.' The man's grin is broad, revealing slightly crooked teeth. He smells vaguely of vetiver and shag tobacco, a combination she can't help finding strangely alluring. If she hadn't already found her master, she'd be curious to learn whether he was single.

'Dan. Glad you could make it. Matilda, this is Daniel Morison. We used to work together in the English department at Leicester. He's faculty head there now. Dan, this is Matilda.'

Nothing more in the way of introduction, which surprises her. The stranger now shaking her hand can't possibly know she is his friend's submissive; this side of their relationship has always been kept a sworn secret between them.

'Do sit down, Dan.'

Daniel accepts the invitation, making himself comfortable in the one available armchair. She wondered why her master had settled himself among a group of three chairs; it's becoming clear this is not going to be the cosy tête-à-tête she'd envisaged when she received his e-mail.

'So, how are things?' Daniel asks. 'I bumped into Maurice a couple of weeks ago and he said you were in Boston ...'

The two men launch into a conversation peppered with names and references to past incidents that mean nothing to her but seem to amuse the pair of them greatly. They only break off when the waitress arrives to take Daniel's order for a glass of Merlot, before returning to the anecdote they're sharing. All the while, she sits patiently, sipping her wine. He hasn't given her permission to join in and, even if he had, there's nothing at all she could add.

At last, he seems to remember she's there. 'So, Matilda. I believe that before Dan arrived you were just about to show me whether you'd complied with the dress code.'

He'd implied nothing of the sort. It's another part of their ritual with which she's becoming very familiar over the years – the raising of her skirt to reveal the tops of the stockings he loves so much, proof she's followed his instructions to the letter – but it's always been conducted in private. She'd make a strong objection, if it wasn't for the fact that the thought of submitting to him in front of an invited audience is making her even wetter.

'Didn't realise they had a dress code for women here,' Daniel interjects. He smiles at Matilda in conspiratorial fashion. 'Though you wouldn't be the first person they'd caught out, believe me. This isn't my tie; they found it for me because I didn't have one on when I arrived.' He waggles the end of the tie at her. It's a sober, black and grey striped affair that doesn't go with anything else he's wearing. Which makes it no different to the rest of his outfit.

Her master shakes his head. 'I don't think the club knows anything about this, and, if they did, they'd probably make it compulsory for all their female staff. You see, Matilda's dress code applies to her underwear as much as to anything else.'

Daniel's eyes widen. He grasps the implications with lightning speed, if the way he's shifting in his seat as though his baggy trousers have grown a size too small for him is any indication.

'So, Matilda, are you ready for your inspection?'

Her eyes can't help but dart round the room. Fortunately, the only man she can see is some old duffer reclining on the brown leather chesterfield close to the fire, snoring gently, a crumpled copy of the *Telegraph* clutched to his blazer-clad chest. Everyone else must have retired to the dining room for plates of steak and kidney pudding and spotted dick.

Satisfied her little display won't be seen by prying eyes, she replies, 'Yes, sir.'

'Very good.' As she begins to rise to her feet, he adds, 'Don't stand up, girl, there's no need.'

27

She should find his use of the term 'girl' patronising and unnecessary, but it simply causes her pussy to cream more strongly. And he isn't being kind to her by telling to remain seated. Hiking up her tight skirt the required distance is difficult enough when she's standing; doing so sitting down is next to impossible, involving a wriggling manoeuvre that slows the process to a humiliating crawl.

Not a word is spoken, two pairs of eyes riveted to her legs as her stockinged thighs appear, inch by agonising inch. She's all too aware of the wetness between her legs, causing the damp and clinging crotch of her knickers to slip between her lips as her backside writhes against the seat of her chair.

At last, the skirt is high enough that the thick dark welts of her stockings appear beneath its hem. Any higher, and she'll be giving them glimpses of her suspender straps and pussy lips bisected by a strip of soaking wet silk.

'Should have known you were a stockings man,' Daniel comments. She can't lift her eyes to meet his gaze, or that of her master.

'Of course,' he replies. 'First thing I did when I started fucking Matilda was make her ditch those nasty, cheap tights she used to wear.' He tosses the word into the conversation with casual abandon, knowing how delight-fully shameful she finds it to have their relationship and the things they do together described in such crude terms. 'Would you like to see what else goes with them?'

She can't believe he's extended such an offer, but the word that would call a halt to all of this remains unspoken. There's no point pretending she doesn't want this. She's always wondered quite how far she'd be prepared to go in following her master's instructions, and it seems to be quite a lot further than she ever believed. Why else would her fingers fly back to the hem of the skirt, ready to push it up further if Daniel accepts the invitation?

It's Daniel who hesitates, as though he isn't sure whether her master is joking or not. 'Are you sure?' he asks.

'I wouldn't say it if I didn't mean it, Dan. You know me.'

Those words are all the assurance Daniel needs. With a little, jerking nod, he signals his desire to see her underwear. Taking a breath, she hitches up her skirt until it's past her stocking tops and her partly covered bum cheeks make contact with the smooth, worn leather of the chair beneath her.

'Oh, very nice. Very nice indeed,' Daniel murmurs.

She looks round, cheeks flushing red. Nothing has changed. The duffer still snoozes on the chesterfield, the antique clock still ticks on the mantelpiece, the room still smells of stewed prunes and old money. But it feels as though a thick pane of glass somehow separates her from what's happening around her. By revealing her underwear to her master's friend, she has removed herself to a place where the normal rules of behaviour no longer apply.

'If you'd like to take a closer look, she'll remove those knickers for you,' her master informs Daniel helpfully. 'You've probably realised by now that Matilda and I don't exactly have an orthodox relationship. She's my submissive, and she follows my instructions because it makes both of us happy, even though she might look like she's dying of embarrassment right at this moment.' He takes a mouthful of whisky, savouring its taste, even though the ice cubes have melted down almost to nothing. 'All you have to do is give her the command.'

Daniel beams like a small child who's been given permission to open his Christmas presents early. 'Matilda, take your knickers off.' Excitement makes his voice crack halfway through the sentence but, though he doesn't possess any of her master's natural authority, she still obeys him. It's not his reaction she's interested in as she reaches up and awkwardly tugs down her underwear, thighs pressed tightly together so she doesn't reveal any more of her pussy than she has to. What concerns her is the approval in her master's eyes. As she bares herself on the instructions of a man she's never met before, he's gazing at her with something that looks very like pride.

Knowing she's pleasing him makes it easier for her to pull the French knickers all the way off, making sure they don't snag on one of her heels. She holds the damp scrap of material awkwardly in her hand, waiting for her next instruction. It isn't long in coming.

'I don't think Daniel can see what he really wants to. Open your legs, Matilda.'

'Sir, I –' Part of her still can't believe this is really happening. What will happen if the waitress walks past and sees her with her wet, needy cunt exposed? Because it is needy, she can't deny that. She's been desperate to come since the moment she received the e-mail, but without his express permission she will continue to remain tense and frustrated.

'I'm waiting, girl.'

That word is the trigger, prompting her to let her thighs loll apart. Daniel's gaze flickers from her blushing face to her newly revealed sex, shaved so that only a strip of hair remains, as per the dress code.

'Does she feel as good as she looks?' Daniel asks.

'Why don't you find out?'

That's how easy it is to give her to another man, if only for a few moments. Daniel comes close, crouching down on the floor so he can get a close-up view of her clit, the shining pearl pushing free from its covering hood. He puts his fingers to his mouth, wetting them with a sweep of his tongue, then presses them to her pussy. The merest contact is enough to have her hanging on the brink of orgasm, afraid she'll lose all control and come before she's allowed. *If*, she reminds herself, she's allowed.

'Easy, easy,' Daniel soothes, changing his tack so that now two fingers push up into her hole. Moving away from her clit dulls the strong, shivery sensations, making it a little easier to hold back, but even so the steady in-and-out fucking motion soon has her humping her arse against the seat. When she left the office, she had no idea she'd find herself in a scene like this, being played with by a stranger under the watchful eye of her master, but she feels crazily alive. Only he can make her feel like this, and when she comes, creaming around the fingers of his friend, it'll be for him and him alone.

But first she has to negotiate her orgasm. Though there's no attempt at negotiation in the breathless pleas she utters as Daniel's thumb brushes over her clit, this time with serious intent. 'Sir, I need to come. Please may I come?'

For a moment, she fears he may refuse, frustrating her even further, but he tells her, 'Since you ask so nicely, girl ...'

That's all the permission she needs. Closing her eyes, she surrenders to the rising pressure, pussy muscles clenching tight round Daniel's thick fingers as she comes. Though she tries to be as quiet as she can, mindful that there might be onlookers, she can't prevent a strangled gasp escaping her lips. The noise is enough to wake the duffer, who looks around for a moment before deciding nothing is amiss and returning to his slumbers.

When Daniel withdraws his fingers, slick with her juices, it seems to break the spell. At her master's command, she eases her skirt back down to a respectable level, though her knickers remain bunched in her hand.

'Oh, Robert, you've got a treasure here.' Daniel's tone is pure envy. 'If you ever get tired of her …'

Her master shakes his head. 'I couldn't give my girl away. Well, not for ever. But if you want to borrow her from time to time …' He smiles at her, giving her a moment to let the idea sink in. 'Have you ever been to Leicester, Matilda?'

'No, sir.'

'I'll keep that in mind. London's a fine city, but sometimes it's nice to have a change of scene at weekends. Though, of course, we'll have to find some way of ensuring that even when you're in Daniel's charge you adhere to the dress code.'

He gives her hand a squeeze, his touch communicating his pride in her display of submission and the love he feels for her. Then he signals to the waitress, indicating that he'd like a fresh round of drinks, as casual as though they'd simply been discussing academic matters.

She has the impression life is about to get very interesting indeed, but, as long as it makes her master happy, she wouldn't want it any other way.

Corporate Punishment
Kat Black

'Wider.'

Arms clasped behind her back, knees stinging where they dig into the coarse twisted fibres of her office carpet, Cate obeys the order without hesitation.

Regardless of the muffled buzz of activity coming from beyond the closed door at her back and the risky choice of location, her blindfolded world is reduced to nothing but the man standing in front of her. Her awareness is narrowed to the commanding tone of his voice, the peppery scent of his arousal, the wet, velvet-on-steel glide of his thick cock between her lips.

'Deeper.'

The strong hands grasping her head shift their grip to the back of her skull. Fingers fist in her hair and pull, leaving her with no option but to comply. Not that her obedience is in question.

Hot and hard, the erection invading her mouth forces forward. From above, a hiss of pleasure sounds at the same instant as the swollen head lodges in the back of her throat.

Too much! Her gag reflex activates and a series of strangled noises escape as she struggles for breath. For a long moment those hands hold her fast while the contracting spasms close tight around the wide tip of the cock. Then the pressure eases as they release to let her pull back, gasping, choking, eyes watering.

'Shh.' Accompanied by a soothing sound the hands move to frame her face, gentle now as they tilt it chin upwards, thumbs wiping at the tears trickling from beneath her blindfold in a gesture of impossible tenderness. 'Good girl.'

No sooner has the worst of her coughing subsided than the touch hardens again, once more taking charge and positioning her to allow the erection to push all the way back in past her still gasping lips – slowly, inexorably, stuffing her mouth full of hot, hard cock.

Cate moans and shudders, stretching her jaw wide and opening her throat to accommodate the unyielding size, even as she squeezes her thighs tight, seeking to ease the fire pulsing between them. Her nipples ache where they've been left exposed to the air-conditioned room, her bra and half-unbuttoned shirt roughly anchored beneath her breasts. The puckered buds stand to full attention, tingling in anticipation of a touch that never seems to come.

She's been burning for ever, it seems – kept at fever pitch while the man at whose feet she kneels takes his time establishing his absolute authority, reducing her to nothing more than this quivering heap of want. By contrast, his voice and actions remain cool and composed as he toys with her, taking what pleasure he desires, exactly as he desires it.

More tears escape to track down Cate's cheeks, this time born of frustrated desire as the slow, torturous pace suddenly becomes more than she can bear. She's waited too long for this. She needs him to use her fast and hard, needs to feel the unfettered power of him bucking and surging and fucking her mouth until his control shreds and in a frenzy he comes undone.

Desperation pushes her to rebel, and in spite of knowing better she dares to unclasp her stiff arms and grab him by the hips. Fingers curling and nails biting into the fine wool of his suit trousers, she seeks to spur the muscled flesh beneath into increased action.

For all the good it does her.

'Catherine,' comes the warning, deep and disapproving, while the powerful glutes beneath her fingertips continue to flex in measured fashion despite her frantic urgings. The cock thrusting into her mouth maintains its infuriating rhythm of perfect pace and control.

Bastard. She'd known he'd be this good.

From the moment their eyes had locked and their wills had clashed across the polished expanse of the conference table days earlier, Cate knew James Grey – CEO of predatory acquisitions giant Greyco Holdings – to be a masterful Dominant, just as he had recognised the sexual submissive in her. Never an easy thing to spot when she's on the job. Swimming alongside the suited sharks in the corporate tank as she does, she's careful not to reveal anything that might be taken for weakness. If only they could understand the half of it – the strength and courage it requires to surrender control, to give yourself over to the mercy of another.

James Grey understands. Right from the first thrilling meeting when they'd shaken hands as opposing equals, there'd been no doubting their respective carnal natures. And as they'd gone head to head in a professional capacity, there'd been no question that things would end up getting very personal indeed.

Knowing full well that every victory gained against him in their negotiations would ultimately result in her punishment hadn't stopped Cate from picking at and unravelling every loose thread she could find in the aggressive Greyco takeover proposal. Quite the opposite, in fact.

Each forced capitulation had won her hard looks that promised retribution and left every hair on her body standing on end. For days, the electric current of their double-layered power games had sizzled like a slow-burning fuse right beneath the oblivious noses of their colleagues and had her walking away from the table limp at the end of each afternoon.

And now, after thrashing out a revised deal and leaving the fine tuning of the contracts to their legal teams, here they finally are – concluding business in their own particular fashion. Cate's only glad that, having shadowed her in stern silence from the boardroom to her office, James Grey had at least taken the time to lock the door behind him before unzipping his trousers and setting about teaching her how little he likes to compromise.

With his silk tie rendering her blind, and his belt buckle digging sharply into her forehead each time he drives his cock deep into her throat, it's certainly a lesson that's being well taught. Cate offers up a muffled moan of pleasure, the sound vibrating along his rigid shaft and causing it to twitch against her tongue. Encouraged by the reaction, she releases her clawing grip on his buttocks and attempts to burrow her fingers into the opening of his flies, ready to squeeze the climax right out of his balls.

'Enough.' James Grey pulls away and, catching her under the arms, hauls her to her feet. Closing a firm hand over the back of her neck, he propels her forward until her thighs meet the glass edge of her desk and pushes her face down across it.

Cate cuts off a shocked cry as her naked breasts press into the cold surface, mindful of the office full of workers on the other side of the door.

'Quiet,' James Grey orders, hands already hiking her skirt up around her waist to expose the tiny white thong that matches her bra. His fingers brush over her skin as he pulls the scant little underpants down over her flesh-coloured hold-ups and off over one patent court shoe at a time. 'Arms behind your back.'

She moves to do as she's told, ears picking up the telltale rattle of his belt buckle loosening followed by the whisper of leather gliding over wool.

Heart pounding, she bows her spine, pushing her arse cheeks up into the air. Straining to hear his next move-ment, she hardly dares to breathe in anticipation of feeling the first fiery lick of the strap.

But as James Grey moves up behind her and begins to wind the belt around her clasped arms instead – binding her wandering hands tight – she realises he's still a long way from giving her what she needs. A little sob of exasperation escapes her lips.

'Surely you didn't think this was going to be about you, did you, Catherine?' James Grey asks, tone slightly mocking as he secures the belt with a final sharp tug. 'Not after all the extra trouble and expense your clever negotiating skills have just put me to?'

Proud as she may be with the successful outcome of

her boardroom wrangling, Cate knows now is not the time to gloat. 'No, sir.'

'Good. Because as far as I'm concerned, you've already had far more from me than you deserve. It's past time that I had something back. Now spread those legs so I can see all of you.'

Flushing with a contrary mix of shame and brazen delight, she presents the aching, wet centre of her need to him, planting her feet so wide apart that her thighs tremble with the effort. Despite not being able to see a thing, she can almost *feel* the intensity of his gaze raking over her intimate flesh and imagines she makes a pretty picture, all trussed up, damp and vulnerable. She gives a wriggle in the hope of luring him forward for a touch.

The moments tick by, further charging the already tense silence of the room, but still James Grey doesn't come forward to touch her. Soon, the sound of muffled movement behind her suggests that he's touching himself instead, and Cate expels a long breathy moan at the mental image she has of those long, strong fingers wrapped around his own cock, pumping and paying homage to her intimate display.

'You have a very fuckable looking arse, Catherine,' he observes at last with a roughened edge to his baritone. 'Tight and sweet. I wonder how easily I'd fit?'

Oh God, not very easily at all to judge by how big he'd felt in her mouth. 'Please,' she begs, circling her hips, desperate for him to give it a try – ready to weep if he doesn't.

'Excuse me?' James Grey's voice moves closer.

'Please, *sir*,' Cate amends in an instant, realising she's forgotten her manners in a haze of lust.

'That's better. But please, what, Catherine? What exactly is it that you're asking me for?'

She feels the brush of his suit and the heat of his body against the back of her naked thighs as he moves in close. 'P-please find out how easily you'd fit, sir.' She pushes back, blindly seeking contact until a hand clamps down over her bound arms and holds her immobile.

'You want me to fuck you?' James Grey asks as he brings the head of his cock to nudge against the puckered entrance of her anus. 'Here?'

Shuddering, rendered speechless by anticipation, Cate nods and feels James Grey begin to push forward, exerting just enough pressure to begin stretching the taut little opening, making her gasp at the stinging sensation.

'I don't think so.' He pulls back, cutting short the dark erotic thrill, leaving Cate to bite off a cry of impotent outrage, her trapped fists clenching in their bonds.

James Grey laughs.

'Perhaps here, instead?' He guides his erection down to the moist, welcoming entrance to her vagina. Pushing forward again, he this time allows the head of his cock to slip a little way inside before he stops. It's a tease – not nearly enough, yet almost more than she can stand. Her internal muscles contract around the width and hardness of him, keen to suck him deeper. But of course he refuses to give her what she needs most.

'Maybe later,' he says, 'or maybe not at all. Although I have to admit you're very tempting, Catherine.' He slips a hand between their bodies and explores her slick folds. 'And very bad. Just how long have you been wet for me?'

'All week, sir,' she gasps as he runs a fingertip around where their bodies join, tracing the sensitive outward bulge of her vulva. 'All week.'

'And what have you done about it?' The hand clamped over her arms moves, transferring its heavy grip to the back of her neck. She feels the weight of James Grey cover her as he leans low over the length of her spine. 'Have you touched yourself?' he asks in an almost-whisper, his breath fanning her ear and tickling her nostrils with the scent of coffee as his fingers stroke expertly between her legs. 'Like this?'

'Yes,' Cate breathes, awash on a sea of pleasure. Need had driven her to take matters into her own hands numerous times, but never once had her own fantasy-fuelled touches felt anything as good as the reality of his.

'Did you make yourself come?' He begins to circle a single fingertip in an outline around her clitoris.

'Yes ... yes, sir.'

'You should know better than that,' he admonishes, letting his finger slow to a standstill. 'I'm disappointed in you, Catherine.'

Afraid that the wicked touch will be withdrawn altogether and leave her to die a slow and torturous death, Cate wriggles again and pleads. 'I'm sorry, sir. Please. I couldn't help myself. I was thinking of you ... of the things I could see that you wanted to do to me.'

The hand at her neck shifts higher into her hair, bunching a handful tight enough to sting her scalp. 'How very presumptuous. And tell me, is this what you saw, Catherine?' James Grey's touch starts up again between her legs. 'My intent to command you, punish you, own you?'

'To master me, yes, sir. And ... and I couldn't wait.'

'Perhaps you need a lesson in self-control.' The grip in her hair twists and tightens, pulling her neck taut. Around and around the finger circles – so clever, so close, but never quite touching the magic spot. 'Perhaps now's a good time to teach you how to wait.'

Pinned at his mercy, Cate squirms, every movement causing James Grey's semi-impaled cock to rub against her sensitive inner walls. The torment is as exquisite as heaven and as maddening as hell.

And it goes on, and on, until she's more than ready to explode. 'Please,' she pants, straining and wriggling in an attempt to shift that finger and cock to where she needs them.

'No.'

She can hear the smile in James Grey's voice as he continues as he wills – his touch electric, his body holding hers captive, his breath growing harsher, rushing against her cheek.

'Please, sir,' she whimpers when another minute passes and her struggles increase. She's so close yet still so far.

'No.'

'Fuck …' Cate sobs after several more interminable moments. 'Please! Please, let me come for you.'

Mercifully, that finger edges closer to her clit, brushing the very edge of the swollen nub. It's enough. '*Ohthankyouthankyouthankyou*,' she gushes as the unbearable tension in her pelvis unfurls, blossoming into the soft imminence of release.

Drawing tight, her entire body stills then begins to shake. At the very moment she reaches the tipping point, James Grey removes his touch.

'I said no,' he growls into her ear. Clamping a palm over her mouth he thrusts forward with enough force to lift her toes off the ground, filling her with the rigid length of his erection. At the same time there is a knock on the door, just audible over Cate's muffled cry, and the world comes crashing back in.

'Excuse me, Ms Alexander?' Her PA's voice sounds through the door. 'I've just had a call from the boardroom to say that the contracts are ready for signature.'

The palm covering her mouth lifts away but Cate's in no fit state to offer an immediate reply. James Grey does it for her. 'Thank you, Emma. Tell them we're on our way.'

Appearing calm and composed as ever, he stays buried inside Cate's trembling, tightly strung body while he sets about removing her bindings and blindfold. She squints against the harsh light as her eyes adjust and groans a pitiful sound of loss when he finally drags the hard thick length of his erection out of her. Limp-limbed, she struggles to push herself upright as she hears the rustle and zip of clothing from behind. Then James Grey is there with his strong, capable hands on her.

Hauling her around to face him, he uses efficient actions to pull down her skirt and straighten her bra and top, taking care of the buttons himself when her fingers prove too shaky to be of much use. While Cate focuses on smoothing the tangles from her hair and regaining some semblance of a professional outer demeanour, he wipes away any traces of mascara-stained tear-tracks and uses a thumb to tidy her lipstick-smeared mouth.

Finished, James Grey steps back, sharp eyes sweeping over her, double-checking every detail of her appearance as he sees to his own final adjustments. He can't be at all comfortable, crammed back into his trousers like he is, but, a true master of control, he doesn't seem to spare it a thought as he bends down to scoop up the damp scrap of her thong lying discarded at his feet.

'This is far from over, Catherine,' he says, straightening and giving her a knee-knocking look. 'And before we're finished, it's going to give me great pleasure to gag your cries for mercy with these pretty little things,' he promises, letting the item of underwear dangle between them for a moment before tucking it into the inner breast pocket of his jacket.

Giving her knees no time to recover their strength, he strides to the door, unlocks and opens it. Standing back, he motions for Cate to precede him. 'After you, *Ms Alexander*.'

On shaky legs she walks ahead of him, the slick reminder of her unfulfilled desire evident with every step. By the time they enter the boardroom, however, she's once again wearing her cool corporate mask and gives not the slightest indication that she's bare-arsed and slippery-thighed beneath her impeccably tailored skirt.

It takes no time at all to have the amended contracts signed but to Cate every second seems like an eternity as she tries not to squirm in her chair. The instant the last 'i' has been dotted and 't' crossed, she's the first person on her feet, desperate to get herself behind the nearest lockable door to sneak some blessed relief before James Grey can get his hands on her again. Confident of her escape in the crowd, she heads for the door at a brisk pace.

'Just a moment, Ms Alexander.' The voice halts her

in her tracks a mere step from freedom. There's nothing to stop Cate making an excuse and running for it – nothing but the fine steel thread that runs through that tone and wraps as effectively as iron shackles around her ankles.

She swivels on the spot to face James Grey, who flashes a smile to the room in general. 'If the rest of you will excuse us –' his gaze narrows in on Cate as he pats a seemingly absent hand over the breast pocket of the jacket '– Ms Alexander and I have one last item of business to conclude.'

Cate orders herself not to blush as she wonders whether anyone will see through the unusual request, but of course, even if they have their suspicions, no one is likely to question a man of James Grey's standing. Remaining rooted to the spot by the door, she offers nods and words of congratulation as everyone files out past her. Beneath the composed façade her heart is pounding, leaving her light-headed as she ponders the exquisite torments to come. Between her legs she can feel the echo of her pulse throbbing hard and heavy behind her clitoris.

Try as she might to resist the urge, her gaze flicks again and again to the conference table, where James Grey is busy gathering up his papers, ignoring her presence. He waits until every last person has gone before standing.

'Lock the door, Catherine, and come here.'

She swallows and reaches out to flip the latch, jumping

at the unexpectedly loud click it makes. Turning back towards him, she sees James Grey's hands are unbuckling his belt once more. She closes her eyes and surrenders to the shiver of anticipation that runs through her. When she opens them again she finds he has the belt folded double in one fist, his other hand is pulling her crumpled thong from his pocket, and the look in his eye says he's done waiting for her.

She crosses the room with quick strides and comes to a halt in front of him.

'Open your mouth,' James Grey orders and she obeys. 'Unfortunately, this is neither the time nor the place to finish things off properly,' he tells her as his fingers begin pushing the wad of her underpants between her lips. 'However, I have a room booked at the Markham tonight. Be there at nine.'

Cate, the musky taste of her own desire on her tongue, breath rushing in and out of her nostrils, blood gushing in her ears, nods.

'In the meantime, I'm going to leave you with a little taste of things to come. Just enough so that every time you sit down this afternoon you'll be reminded of me and the cost of the payback I'm going to exact. Pull your skirt up around your waist.'

Again, Cate obeys without hesitation, her eyelids fluttering shut when James Grey inserts a hand between her legs and thrusts his middle finger deep up inside her.

'And I'll take just enough of this to remind *me* of how much you're going to like paying that price.' He slides the finger out with slow deliberation and raises it to his mouth, his eyes locked on Cate's as he makes a show of sucking at her glistening juices. A fresh wash of warmth floods her pelvis as she watches his pupils dilate.

'Up on the table and on all fours, now.' Before he's finished issuing the order, Cate's already halfway there. Once she's in position, James Grey strokes a soothing palm once over each smooth white buttock cheek in turn, drawing a muffled moan from behind her gag.

'Not another sound.' James Grey punctuates the warning with the first stinging slap of his belt, catching Cate unawares. 'And so help you if you move a single muscle again before I say you can, Catherine.'

Eyes drifting closed and a blissful smile stretching her lips, Cate draws in a deep breath and braces herself.

Yours
(A Letter to Willow Sears)
Willow Sears

Dear Mistress,

I have done something so dirty I can't even bring myself to tell you about it. If I try, the words will just stick in my throat, barbed by the last remnants of dignity that I have left in me. They are such little words really, but they carry the weight of unmentionable shame that would empty me, purging me of any remaining esteem. I know if I stay silent you will simply spank the truth from me. I know if your open palm cannot make me, you will send down the hard paddle or even the cane across the fleshiest part of my wobbling bottom, across the tops of my thighs, or even against my poor desperate quim until the words flow from me in a shivering release of utter ignominy and disgrace.

I should have expected punishment for admitting I liked Selena, but I cannot lie to you ever. She is beautiful and you know it. The first time I saw her I tried to face the wall so I couldn't see how delicious her big white arse looked squeezing out of the circle cut into her rubber catsuit. But you know all my weaknesses and forced me to turn around to look. You made me watch her take her rubber whip to Mimi's huge tits and lash them until her nipples were so long and swollen they looked fit to burst. You made me watch her fill the slave's pussy with cake, and have the girl frig for us and lick her fingers clean of cream and chocolate. You knew that I would see the joy of cruelty spread her wide mouth into a smile, and then see those same lips kiss poor Mimi so tenderly afterwards, just as you do to me. You know I have no love left in me for anyone other than you, but still you sent me to Selena to receive my chastisement for the slight of noticing her, when I should only have eyes for you.

* * *

I remember the last time you made me admit to liking a girl. It was when you sent me alone to those Spanish classes, telling me I had to speak the language with your fluency if I wanted to join you, should you ever return there. There was something about our tutor Isobel that caught my attention. Her eyes were green like your own. She taught us with a soft voice and joined the giggles at our terrible mispronunciations. I could not help but be enlivened by her smile. Her black hair was pulled back tightly and her little round glasses gave her a look of sweet innocence at odds with the low-cut tops that she wore, hinting at her heavy breasts and deep cleavage. She wore a bright silver cross on a delicate chain, the sign of her faith hanging precariously and threatening to be sucked down at any moment into the chasm of her bosom.

All of this I told you, remember? They were just inno-cent remarks but as soon as they fell from my lips I knew I had spoken out of turn. Your lip curled and you spat in my face as you always do when I have caused your ire. You made me crouch down with my cheek resting against your spiked boot, and I could feel your whip-tongue tracing lines over my bare back. You asked me if Isobel made me wet. All I said was that she was nice and I liked her, but because of this alone you said that action must be taken. I might have known that your punishment would not be immediate, and that you would take your usual time to plan it carefully. Even though you kept me on the floor for over an hour with my exposed bottom up in the air I should have realised that you only left me there to ponder my fate. I couldn't sleep for thinking about it. I sat in a mute heap outside your bedroom, just in the hope of catching your thoughts. Your silence and inattention burned me for those few days and I would have endured any roasting, any pain or indignity, just to hear your voice. But mental torture is your forte, and I am just so easy for you to ignore.

When you finally did deliver my punishment your preparations turned out to be as meticulous as ever. You had me wear a loose, knee-length skirt and you accompanied me to that final class. Before it started you smuggled me into the toilets and had me bend over in the locked cubicle. You stripped my knickers away and then you took the red lipstick from my bag to prepare me. I shall never forget the extra punishment you threatened me with if I failed to do your bidding that night. You sat right at the front of the classroom knowing I would have to walk past you and be closest to you when the time came. You put me at the back, sitting with my hands beneath my thighs to elevate my weight and with my skirt loose around the seat and not under me, to avoid any smudging. I had to sit like this for half of the lesson.

At precisely eight-thirty as you had previously ordained, with Isobel going through her verb-endings, I got up and silently walked towards her. I stopped two feet short of her and turned to face the class, then looked back over my shoulder at her enquiring face, her mouth still open but her words arrested. Then I bent over, pulled my skirt up over my back and stuck out my naked bottom for her to see. Her eyes widened and there was a collective gasp from the class. I heard her breathe, '*Santa Maria!*' and then the hush fell, quieter than silence, the air reverberating and banging in my ears.

I stuck my backside right out for her as you had instructed. You had shown me in the toilet cubicle exactly how to do it to make it work. Like all the others in the class the tutor was dumbfounded, but only she could see what you had written across my buttocks in bright red lipstick. I watched her virtuous face scanning the words with growing horror, her colour draining as she digested the message written on my godless arse in your firm hand. It said:

'Dildo-fuck my shit hole.'

It was probably the rudest thing she had ever seen. The first two words were written across the very top of my buttocks, where the crease began. The next two were beneath, side by side where my swell is widest, and separated by my deep crack. Below that, just above my inward tuck, the 'h' was on one cheek, while 'le' was on the other. My little round anus, visible in the yawn of my bottom and heavily ringed in red lipstick, provided the 'o' of the final word.

I stayed as I was for thirty endless seconds of frozen time, silently counting them down, the whole room holding its breath. I was desperate to run but I knew you would be timing me too, and ready to pounce if I disobeyed you and pulled up short. When it was finally over, I stood up and covered myself, and then left as calmly as I could, my face burning with my shame and hot tears. You didn't follow me. You made me wait for an excruciating half-hour more, standing by your car until the class was over and the pupils began to file out. I saw them looking and pointing over at me, whispering and laughing. Even now as I type this letter, my hands are shaking at the memory of that humiliation. I wonder if you even remember it.

* * *

So you see why I pleaded my innocence so hard when you accused me of loving Selena. You refused to believe my denials. You said you could clearly see the hunger in my eyes whilst I watched her gloved fist slide into Mimi's young cunt. You said I had involuntarily clutched my own cunt when she had excreted the whipped cream from her fat arse into Mimi's clamped-open mouth. You declared that no bitch had ever before acted with such open contempt for their Mistress. It was, you told me, the most terrible slight you could imagine, and one deserving of the severest retribution. Worse still, you couldn't even be bothered to deal with me yourself, electing to send me to Selena for her to administer your punishment by proxy. I had seen what she did to her girls and you knew it was beyond my tolerance. That was the worst thing: having you send me away. It tore me apart knowing you couldn't even be bothered to raise your hand to me.

I don't suppose you recall that I was confined to my room for nearly a week before you sent me to her. You didn't accompany me on the day. The car took me and deposited me and then drove off, so I knew there was no hope of reprieve. I was met at the back door by Selena's plump black housekeeper, dressed in white lace blouse and striped butcher's apron. She had a face like thunder so she must have known I stood accused of being a wanton, undeserving slave-bitch. She let loose an array of curses in her accented English and grabbed me by the wrist to yank me over the threshold. She then produced a long thin string with a miniature noose tied at one end. She told me to stick out my tongue and she slipped the noose around it, pulling the thread tight to the muscle. The stud through my tongue prevented the noose sliding off and thus she was able to take the string and lead me away without resistance.

On turning I saw that her thick jutting arse was completely bare. Both jiggling buttocks were lined all the way down with a series of narrow, dark, raised welts. She caught me eyeing them and stopped, sticking her rump out at me and pulling me down to force a closer inspection. She informed me if I took one step out of line that day she would personally ruin my botty in such a fashion. She would heat the cane over the flames until it was smouldering, she said, and then coat the wounds in salt and leave me hanging like a ham. I was dragged by the tongue up two flights of stairs, my face ever in peril of disappearing into the chocolate crack of her fat backside. We finally stopped halfway along a red-walled corridor. The housekeeper gave me one last dirty look, sucked her teeth in derision and then released my tongue from the noose. It was a brief if unsettling time in her company, one that made me fear the remainder of the day's proceedings. I was right to.

I knocked at the door before me and a voice inside bade me enter. Selena's bedroom was huge. In front of the big screen at one end there was an area with plump cushions and bolsters scattered on the floor around her decorative chaise. Then the floor stepped up and her divan sat on this raised platform, surrounded by an iron frame with high finials, and covered in rich silks. The walls were decorated in tapestries and fabric hangings in red and gold, and I could smell rose from the fresh petals in the open bowls, and incense from the burners. It could have been the room of an Ottoman princess, except for the two video cameras set up and pointing towards the bed.

Slave-girl Mimi was already on the divan, stripped naked and lying on her back. Her arms stretched up over the pillow and her wrists were secured to the headboard by short gold chains. Her large breasts were flattened to her chest by their own weight. Her dark nipples were still dormant, the teats just visible above the surrounding brown flesh. Her legs were not bound and lay loosely apart, the olive skin of her smooth thighs shining. She lay quietly, but I could tell by the redness and the slick veneer of come that covered her cunt that she had just had it spanked.

Selena brought me a glass of red wine, so large that it held maybe a third of the bottle at once, but I was thankful for anything that would calm my rattling nerves. It smelled of forest fruits and liquorice. It started out tasting sweet, but then an acrid bitterness came through at the end to spoil it. She drank hers with no complaint and encouraged me to drink mine down. Once I had drained the glass she took it and left the room to fill it once more, ignoring my declination. She watched as I drank this too. As her smile spread and the same medicinal tartness burnt my tongue, I knew for certain that she had spiked it.

I was made to watch her films, shot in that very room and in other locations, featuring an assortment of her slave-girls. We watched for maybe an hour. I sipped from a constantly refilled glass of wine as I witnessed her merciless assaults on the variously costumed victims. She was very proud of her work, and gave self-congratulatory comments at some of her more inventive or effective punishments. I, although anaesthetised by the drink, still stiffened with trepidation and shrank into the cushions at her feet.

I watched an on-screen Mimi being whipped by nettles as she licked a girl's bottom. I witnessed the housekeeper getting her scarred fat arse fucked at incredible speed by a thick rubber prick on the end of a pummelling mechanical arm. I saw one anonymous wretch, wearing a grotesque mask in the form of a horse's head, bent over and fucked by Selena wielding some enormous dildo – a brown and suede-soft monster, complete with a ballsack like a round leather purse. She told me it was the stuffed cock of a stallion, but she laughed as she said it, and I didn't know if I should believe her or not. As the films went on, the cries of pain through the speakers grew louder as the beatings and indignities intensified. She could see I was wracked with foreboding.

'Don't worry,' she said, 'I'm not going to lay a single hand on you in anger. Your punishment will come in another way.'

I was glad that she seemed to have taken some guidance from you, but still her words did not allay my fears, because I know well enough that pain comes in many forms.

Do you recall, for instance, the night of that party at The Convent? You had me dress as a cheerleader, in that tight Lycra top and tiny pleated skirt. I put on little socks and white trainers to match, and you gave me the tightest pair of pristine white knickers, saying that you had taken them from a schoolgirl, although they looked brand new to me. You made me use the pussy vacuum to pump myself up and make me extra sensitive, and then you had me squeeze into the knickers, stretching them across my bulge to breaking point. At the party, you made me lift my skirt to every man who came by to show them how big my mound was beneath the taut white cotton.

He stopped and stared, clutching his glass in one thick dry hand. He had the wrinkled skin of a heavy smoker and hair the colour and texture of straw. He leered at me like he owned me. You knew I detested him and that's why you let him touch me. You had me part my thighs as I stood, and his big hand came out and cupped my cunt, so I could feel the scratch of his calloused skin through the fabric. Do you remember what you made me do? You had me piss into my underwear while he held me, so that my stream drenched through and filled his palm before spilling down my thighs and on to the kitchen floor. When I was sopping he pushed the material aside and slid one finger through my flow and right up into my pussy, stirring my wetness inside me, smiling at my discomfort.

Then you made me suck his disgusting thick cock. You told me to take it all in even though he was just some dirty old bastard. You had me gobble and wank his prick like a whore whilst he licked his palm and fingers clean. You even made me take his scalding, filthy spunk into my mouth and swallow it all down, although it made me gag. I thought you would reward me later for being so good. Instead you had me crouch at the foot of your huge bed while you lay there covered in your silk sheets, completely ignoring me. I was naked and on my knees, and you had stuffed my holes with the panties you had taken from those triplet girls at the party, the ones whose fat pale bums you had bent over in a line and fingered one by one, right in front of my eyes.

I watched you pick up the phone and dial. You said only three words but they cut me like any cane. You said:

'Darling, it's me.'

I strained to hear the words spoken to you, to discover what had made you throw off the sheets and masturbate so urgently, but all I could make out was a soft electronic murmur, muffled by your ear. When your gush finally came, you sighed, put down the phone and then turned off the light, leaving me there as if I didn't exist. It ripped at my insides. The pain was complete and agonising, and you hadn't laid a finger on me. Do you even remember that night?

Selena finally turned off the screen and told me to strip for her. When I was naked she led me up to the bed and made me climb on. She had me straddle Mimi, facing her feet, my thighs stretched across her torso and her big tits beneath my bottom. I felt hands at my calves. I looked round to see that my ankles were now strapped and had been secured to the headboard by similar chains to the ones that held Mimi's wrists. Then she was beneath my bottom, and Mimi was gasping. I looked over my shoulder and saw the chained clamps being applied to her swiftly engorging nipples, and Selena pulling on them to increase their growth still further.

The Mistress placed a hand on my forehead and gently pushed back. She took one chain and pulled it up towards my head, stretching Mimi's nipple impossibly until she was able to clip the other end with biting pressure to my earlobe. She repeated the procedure on the other side, so that my bottom was now thrust out and my back arched in. My head was snapped back and my own delicate flesh was painfully connected to Mimi's elongated nipples by the metal lengths, squashing her tit-flesh cosily to my bum cheeks. Then Selena turned on both cameras and left us there, saying that she would return later in the evening.

The position was uncomfortable but I thought I had been let off very lightly. My hands were free to remove the clips, but the evidence would be caught on film, and I couldn't let you see me fail. After another hour I started to feel the pressure in my bladder turning to an ache, and the fluttering tingle in my belly betrayed the first signs of danger. Panic stirred at the first butterfly flurry, and then settled in after the next brief cramp. I tried to draw my bottom in, to squeeze my inner muscles just as you like me to do on your fingers so that I bathe them in my warm flow, but my position prevented all but the smallest of movements. I felt a little sleepy and lost, as if the energy was slowly draining from my body, down from my shoulders and my back, down into my legs where it could exert no control at all. I screwed my eyes shut and was met with the mental image of Selena smiling as I sipped the wine, her desire for me to drink it all down, two whole glasses and much more of it, despite the bitter tinge that made me sure that all was not well.

For one flitting second of hope I wondered if you might come and save me, undo the chains and lead me to safety. Perhaps you had me in mind all the while, and wanted to lift my desperate relief from the siege that my own clenching muscles had imposed. Then I was scared that you *would* come, and witness me on the verge of absolute debasement, and cast me aside in disgust the moment I lost the battle and had to give in to nature. It was a test of endurance and I knew I was destined for defeat. In the end I was glad you left me alone, and I took comfort in the hope that perhaps you were thinking of me during my ordeal.

I fought hard, whimpering as the pressure grew and

my bladder threatened to burst. I knew the ultimate humiliation was approaching, and that it was your will, if only indirectly. I tried to hang on, but in the end the pain was too much, with no end in sight except release. By that time I was crying – huge sobs which only made the cramps worse. Mimi was trying to comfort me, blissfully unaware of what was very soon going to befall her. I prayed that the cameras would run out of film before the moment was captured, but I knew that they would not. I wished above all that my pussy was not crying out so much for attention in this, my darkest hour. But it was.

In the end there was nothing for it except to give in. I didn't warn her. I did what I thought was the only thing I could do: I clutched my pussy and rubbed it as hard as I could, and leant forward and did the same for her, to try and make the ordeal as bearable as possible for us both. She cried out instantly and thrust upwards as the tremors of bliss and the threat of appalling, filthy disgrace surged through me. Then we came together and I heard us both screaming. I was trying to let go and hold on at the same time. My muscles were contracting wildly and it felt like every single nerve-ending in my body, from the top of my head downwards, was being stripped from inside me and dragged out into the air. The release was huge, awful and beautiful.

Even now, I still can't bring myself to tell you what actually happened. I thought that was what this letter was for, but now I come to it, my hand just won't write the words. I don't know if you will want me back if you think my degradation and humiliation are complete. I'm empty, and only you can fill me again. All I ever wanted was to do your bidding, to let you do as you pleased with me. You can again if you will only have me. I know Selena will show you the film and I wish I could tell you myself, but I can't. All I can say is that I did it for you and I hope that my abject shame won't lead you to discard me now, when I need you more than ever. I will sit here waiting, praying for your call, and if you want me you know that I am, as always, truly

Yours.

A Different Kind of Tension
Chrissie Bentley

I knew they were handcuffs the moment I felt the cold metal bite my wrist, as I stretched out one arm to cradle my head. I felt my heart leap in my chest, although whether it was the sudden immobility that startled me most, or the fact that he'd been so gentle all evening, I didn't know. Nor was every thought that now crossed my mind necessarily a pleasant one. 'You've been watching too much *CSI*,' I reassured myself as I tested the strength of the cuffs, but I quickly realised I wouldn't be freeing myself from them any time soon.

Roughly, he grabbed my other arm and yanked it across the bed, to where another set of cuffs was waiting. I wondered how I'd not spotted them earlier, and blamed either the wine or the candlelight or both. And besides,

I had other things to think about. Such as the total transformation in Terry, a quiet, considerate guy with whom I'd been on nodding-acquaintance terms for at least the last six months, and who now crouched menacingly astride me, massaging his cock with exaggerated drama and staring me down with a hungry leer.

* * *

The first time I met him, a girl I was working with brought him along to a party we'd both been invited to, and introduced him as her fiancé. Which, so far as I was concerned, was still the case when I bumped into him this evening, waiting at my usual bus stop.

We said hello, talked till the bus came, then found two seats together before anyone beat us to them. By the time we reached my neighbourhood, which turned out to be his as well, I'd learned that Sara, the cute-in-a-slutty-sort-of-way blonde with whom I first met him, had broken off their engagement; by the time we were about to actually say goodbye, I was agreeing to go for a drink with him. Well, one drink led to several, which led in turn to dinner, which led us back to his place, a cosy one-bedroom apartment with just enough domestic touches around to make it clear that Sara had not been gone long – a couple of weeks, maybe; a month at most.

But the bathroom was clear of any sign of a woman

(the toilet seat was up, for a start), and the first time Terry touched me, our hands inadvertently meeting as we both reached for the wine bottle, he leaped back so apologetically that it was obvious that Sara hadn't simply left him. She'd taken a lot of his self-confidence with her.

'It's all right, it was an accident,' I reassured him, then reached out and took his hand in mine. 'Now, if you'd done that ...' I squeezed his fingers and looked into his eyes, a heavy green that clashed intriguingly with his burgundy shirt. His hand, twice the size of mine, twisted in my grip, and linked fingers with me. He smiled. 'Or that?' His other hand reached for my chin and slowly pulled my face to his, to kiss me tentatively on the mouth. I kissed back, parting my lips to accept his tongue, and sliding both hands under his armpits to clasp his back.

He was a cautious lover, an uncertain lover. Even in the bedroom, with our clothes in a heap on the end of the bed (I was sure they were on the end; they definitely weren't on the chair to the side, which is where they now lay), he moved with a deliberation that was as clumsy as it was gentle, as he gave my pussy little more than a rubbing, and licked my nipples with a puppy-dog tongue. He rolled me on to my back while we kissed, and moved above me; reaching between my legs, I grasped his penis, then guided him slowly inside me – it had to be slowly, for, although I was willing, I was still barely wet.

He lay still for a moment; I could feel my muscles testing the length of his erection, feeling its pulse, surveying its contours, absorbing its heat – and then fluttering in surprise, as he silently shot his load. I caught my breath, searching for one of those stock phrases that we all use when something like that happens. Some girls stick with 'It's OK, it doesn't matter,' but you know what? It does, especially to him. I always prefer to gasp and tell him how much I love the feel of his come inside me, maybe fish a drop or two out on my finger, and slip it into my mouth. It works every time.

But before I could even open my mouth, he started to hump me, his hips pounding into mine as though his dick was as hard as it ever could be, and we were both on the edge of the world's hottest orgasm.

I was surprised, but I played along. He wasn't the first guy to come way too early and hope it hadn't been noticed, although I do sometimes wonder how dense a woman would have to be, to truly remain oblivious to all that had suddenly transpired within her: the explosive influx of a mass of sticky warmth, the pounding on the cervix door that fades and then gives up; and the almost indescribable sensation of a hot rod growing soft. Imagine cramming your mouth with a hard king-size candy bar that suddenly melts on your tongue while squirting hot yogurt into your throat. Now think about how a pussy is at least as sensitive as a mouth, even without the power of taste. But I feigned ignorance, I 'came' ecstatically and for a while we just lay there, my cheek on his chest, content not to speak.

His flaccid length lay on his belly, staring up at me; I stared back, wondering what the chances were of it not rising again tonight, envying the ability that so many men possess, of having sex and then heading straight home. In fact, I was just about to suggest that I should make a move when he placed his hand on the back of my head and began pushing it down towards his lap.

I locked my neck muscles. I've had a lot of practice at this manoeuvre, although it's been a long time since I actually put it into use; not since college, when even making out with a guy seems to convince him that you're gagging to give him head. OK, so Terry and I had certainly gone a lot further than making out, and I'm only half-serious when I insist to myself that I'll only go down on a guy once I know he'll return the favour. But, even as Terry hoisted himself into a sitting position, so that I lost my balance and tumbled, I made sure my head remained in neutral waters, my face looking down his leg. OK, it was definitely time to be going. I moved my arm to cradle my head – and click. I struggled to pull myself out of his grip – and click again.

I was cuffed to the posts at the bottom of the bed, my feet resting on the pillows at the other end. Grabbing one of them, Terry shoved it unceremoniously under my ass, then straddled my stomach, his cock – which was now showing distinct signs of life – sticky between my breasts. He looked down at me and spoke for the first time since we left the front room. 'I tried to ask you nicely. Now I'm telling you.' He held his semi-erection in one hand and pushed it towards my face. 'Suck it.'

Hardening to a dark bruised blue, the head of his penis was flat against my lips, nudging them apart and pressing against my teeth; I could taste my own juices still vibrant on his skin. Slowly I opened my mouth, not wide enough for him to jam himself in, but sufficient to take in most of the bulb. Using my tongue, I mopped it with saliva, then sucked at it, feeling my own thrill of power as his eyes closed and a low groan escaped his lips. He may have been in the driving seat, but I still had some control over the journey.

My hands pulled at the cuffs; if I was going to do this, I'd like do it properly. But they remained trapped, and the movement only alerted Terry. 'Oh no, you're here until I'm finished with you,' he said; then, withdrawing himself from my still stubbornly tightened mouth with a light plop, he commanded, 'Wider. Open it wider.'

I shivered a little. I don't usually get off with a man who plays the master, but Terry did have me at a disadvantage. I obeyed and, for a moment, my jaw just hung, as he held his rod an inch or so away, allowing my nostrils to absorb his scent. Instinctively, I craned my head forward, to take him into my mouth again. He certainly knew how to play this game, I thought, and I felt my own loins quiver warmly as he began to push himself forward, forcing my mouth even wider, scraping against my teeth, pushing my tongue to one side. He wasn't huge, probably no more than five inches, but he had a lot of circumference, a fat, meaty roll of hardness that was bumping against the very back of my mouth. 'Now I'm going to fuck you properly,' he said. 'Like I should have done before.' And, with slow, methodical strokes, he began to do just that, his eyes closed in rapture as he slipped in and out of my mouth.

His hands were caressing his balls; with every thrust, his sac slapped against my chin, reinforcing in my mind the position I was in, at the same time as I felt myself pulsing in time to his movements, finding an excitement in my predicament that even my occasional bondage fantasies had never aroused. If he'd only let me speak for a moment, I thought, I'd tell him what I want him to do: reach behind to touch me, finger me, fist me, anything. And then I heard a door open, footsteps, another voice. And the pulse became a galvanic throbbing through my entire body.

'Who's your friend?' It was a woman. I struggled to place the voice. It was Sara, the fiancée who'd fled, the heartless harpy who broke his heart. What the hell was going on here? For a moment I imagined myself being caught in the middle of some knockdown fight between two bitter ex-lovers, while being reduced to a trophy for one to bait the other one with. But that was before Terry answered her.

'You know who it is. One of those sluts from your whorehouse downtown.'

She leaned over to look at me, her eyes flashing a spark of recognition, but that was all; we'd never been friends, just workmates; I doubted whether she even knew my name. Instead, she went along with what was clearly Terry's fantasy, the embittered whoremaster making free with a rival madame's merchandise. 'Oh, and one of my favourites as well,' she said, pouting. 'Please don't scar her pretty face, I won't earn half as much from her ass if you do.'

Now I could see her more clearly, as she leaned across my sightline to kiss Terry on the mouth, before her bare breasts blotted out their faces, and her hard, protruding nipples sank like plum-brown bullets into his chest. For the moment, his movements had stopped, the merest touch of his hard-on poised against my cheek, a thin, gummy film of spit and pre-come holding it in place. I moved my head slightly to breathe deeply and let my tongue moisten my dry, salted lips.

Sara spoke again. The roles had changed; now she was the leader, and Terry just a lackey who prepared her victims for sacrifice. 'I think it's my turn.' Her hand wrapped around his protesting stiffness, lifted it away from my face. 'You find yourself another hole. This one's mine.' She hoisted herself over the foot of the bed, first one leg and then the other, her naked body directly over my face. 'So tell me, have you ever eaten pussy before?'

At the other end, I could feel rough hands parting my ass cheeks, and Terry's hard knob banging at my anus. 'No, I haven't,' I answered truthfully. I almost added, 'But I thought about it once,' remembering a long-ago weekend that I spent at the shore, but Sara was speaking again. 'I didn't think you had. But I bet you like having yours licked?'

I remained silent. 'Don't you?' she repeated. 'Don't you just love how it feels when a tongue is prying open your lips, tasting your flesh, swirling and moving inside you, hunting out your most secret spots and then drowning in your juices, while you ride their face with your little clitty, till you feel yourself coming and your whole body explodes? Answer me.'

Damn, the girl had a way with words! 'Yes, I love it,' I replied.

'More than you love screwing?'

'Yes.' If it's done right, that was probably true.

'More than you love sucking cock?'

'Yes.' Again, done right.

'Well, if you love it that much …' Her flesh moved closer to me and, for the first time, I realised she'd been in too much shadow before and that she was shaven completely bare, the skin gossamer-soft as it brushed against my mouth, but already wet as her juices leaked from within her. Tentatively, my tongue reached up to touch her, and her labia parted to the lightest touch, her smell flooding my nostrils, making my mouth water for her taste. I let out a moan – I couldn't help myself – and another as Terry finally gave up trying to break into my asshole (the angle was wrong; I knew that from the start), and began sliding his dick down my own dripping pussy, as though it, too, were a tongue taking its first trip to a place it had only ever dreamed of.

Sara's breath was coming in short gasps. Stretching my tongue as far as it would reach, I probed deeper inside her and she, sensing my hungry straining, lowered herself a little further, her liquid lips spreading across my mouth as I carried on licking her, relying upon her own subtle shifts and movements to guide my tongue to where she wanted it to be. My nipples were burning, my hole crying out for Terry to fill it, but he was still teasing, his deepest penetration little more than a nudge, the velvety tip grazing me here, there, everywhere, then slipping away as my body begged for more.

Sara's clit was beneath my tongue now, a firm erection amid the soft flesh, and I wondered how so many men could miss something like that. It wasn't only the difference in texture that made it stand out, but the difference in reaction as well; as my tongue traced its lines around that hard, red knot, Sara's body relaxed into the motion; the moment I actually touched it, though, she tensed until every nerve in her body stood to attention and, the more I nuzzled and suckled that tiny, sweet bud, the tauter her body became.

Her hips were rocking, grinding into my face, but my tongue held its ground, drilling into her most sensitive spot while her internal muscles flexed to a frenzied beat that matched my racing heart. Pursing my lips, I sucked her into my mouth and I heard her cry out. If I could only have moved, I would have thrown her to the ground, then buried my face back into her, pounded her with my fingers while I licked and flicked and sucked and fucked her with my mouth; instead, I let my face do the fucking, driving my tongue as deep as I could, while jarring her clit with the tip of my nose.

Terry was inside me now, fucking me properly, his hands pawing at my breasts. Once I felt him tongue and then bite at one of my nipples, but the pain just made me more determined to give his fiancée (I think we can safely assume that they were still together after all, no matter what kind of line he'd spun me before) the kind of orgasm that he would never be capable of granting her.

I bucked my hips against him, driving him towards his own grand finale, so that maybe he'd leave us alone, then time stood still as Sara's body froze. I sensed, rather than heard, the cry building within her; knew that her moment was just inches away. For a split second, I was uncertain how to react; should I stop what I was doing, let her grind out her own final instructions to my mouth? Or should I do what I would want to have done to me, if the positions were ever to be reversed? As I fully intended they should be?

My tongue lashed out, my lips sucked, my teeth nipped and, as Sara came once, twice, three times in lightning-fast succession, my own body lurched into orgasmic hyperspace, every inch of my skin screaming in triumph as I came not simply with my sopping cunt but with my entire soul.

I felt a hot splash on my stomach and breasts; Terry, too, had finally climaxed, pulling sharply out of me as his own juices peaked, and splashing a flood of seed across my torso. Sara, her voice a bare whisper between her purring gasps, commanded him to clean it up, and I felt his rough tongue flicking over my body as he obeyed her; as everybody, I imagined, would want to obey her.

She slipped off me, her vagina tracing a thick smear of love juice across my cheek as she moved. 'Now feed it to her,' she snapped. 'It's what you wanted to do before, isn't it?'

Terry nodded eagerly, leant forward and slipped his tongue, coated in his own come, into my mouth. I fastened my lips to his offering, sucked it in and swallowed it down; accepted, too, his dripping, sticky fingers, then obediently lapped at the end of his damp, drooping cock, my mouth so saturated by both his and her juices that I scarcely even felt its last gasps dribbling on to my tongue.

Patiently, I rattled the handcuffs. 'Any chance of getting out of these?' I asked. 'Being as nothing seems to be happening that I need to be held down for.'

Sara nodded and Terry produced the keys from where he'd dropped them, beneath the bed. As he unlocked me, I stretched each arm luxuriously; both had all but fallen asleep, and both were going to ache like hell tomorrow. I suddenly noticed that I was parched. 'And a drink?' I asked. Again Sara nodded, and Terry dutifully reached for one of the wine glasses.

'Get her something fresh,' Sara said, tutting. 'Wine? Water? Soda?'

'Soda would be great.' Naked, Terry left the room. 'Nice little set-up you guys have here.'

Sara smiled. 'Some people aren't keen, but you can usually spot them early enough ... right around the time the first handcuff goes on.'

'I was surprised. I thought Terry –'

'You thought Terry was too busy trying to get his cock sucked,' she interrupted. 'No, he's good at what he does. All I have to do is make the place look nice.' She indicated the candles. 'Pick up a little – don't want to get stains on those four-hundred-dollar sweaters, you know – and, of course, get the playthings in place to begin with.' I laughed; then, as Terry returned and handed me a Pepsi, I asked her, 'So will there be another performance tonight?'

Sara shrugged. 'I don't see why not. Terry's quite the stallion when he wants to be.' She reached out to squeeze his soft penis and, as she released it, I saw it twitch a nod of gratitude. I repeated the gesture, squeezing the bulb between forefinger and thumb, feeling new life already start to flow. 'I think we're definitely on for another round,' I said; then, leaning forward, I managed to lock both of Sara's arms into the handcuffs before she even knew what was happening.

She laughed. 'The boot is on the other foot, I see. Well, don't worry, I love pussy, too.'

'I'm sure you do,' I told her. 'But I've not quite decided which I prefer.' Kneeling at Terry's feet, I took him slowly into my mouth once again, only this time it was on my terms, sucking when I wanted to suck, licking when I wanted a change, allowing every muscle of my mouth to work at restoring him to full length and strength. Only then did I release him – just a little reluctantly, because a well-oiled prick has a texture all its own – and I strad-dled Sara's face, lowering myself over her and tensing delightfully as her tongue made its first entry, instinctively travelling to the areas where, after Terry's earlier efforts, I felt a little sore.

My hands clenched her tits, kneading them in tight, tender fists, feeling her nipples like acorns against my palm. I squeezed and twisted them, slipping my fingertips into the crease between chest and breast and raising them, crushing them, feeling Sara squirm beneath my rough grip. Terry moved down, to take up what was evidently his usual position between the prone girl's legs, but I told him to halt.

'No. Come here,' I told him. 'I want you to fuck us both.' From between my thighs, I heard Sara try to speak, but I already enveloped her mouth, revelling in the feather-light touch of her silken chin and cheeks. I had never imagined how glorious cunnilingus could feel without a man's tough stubble to scratch at my softest skin, even as his mouth worked to thrill it.

Terry looked sheepish. 'Sara doesn't like to do that,' he mumbled, and I wondered, is that how the pair of them developed this whole routine in the first place, just so Terry could get a blow job without his fiancée getting her lips wet? 'Well, it looks like we're all going to try something different tonight,' I answered and, reaching out, I pulled his hardness towards my pussy as it writhed above Sara's darting tongue, and wrapped my arms around his back to hold him steady. 'Now do it.'

It was an almost impossible position, not only

physically but also for his poor cock, slipping between two inviting holes, unable to decide which one it wanted most. And so it dipped and rose, slid and slithered, one moment burying its head deep inside me, the next pulling out to delve into her mouth. I imagined how Sara must be feeling, as her tongue first lolled on to him, recoiling at the immediate shock of his hard and musky flesh, but fascinated by it as well, flicking back to check it out again, and lingering longer every time.

Very quickly, I realised that, in terms of actual physical pleasure, neither Sara's tongue nor Terry's penis was ever going to bring about a repeat of the orgasm that I'd already experienced – not in this position, anyway. But that, I decided, was no longer the point. I reached down between my legs, and began rubbing the top of his shaft, pressing it down on to Sara's mouth with my fingers, as I surrendered my claim on her tongue.

I slipped to one side. Terry instantly took my place, brushing his free-flowing pre-come around her cheeks and lips, taunting her with the promise of entry, before withdrawing to dance once again on her nerve-ends. Then, he plunged himself into her mouth, fucking it like he'd fucked mine, oblivious to the grunts of protests that rose within her throat; for he knew, just as I did, that for all her reluctance she needed him inside her; that, even as she tried to complain, her mouth was stretching wide to take him further in, driving him towards orgasm with teeth and tongue and the force of her sunken-cheeked sucking.

Her eyes were closed, her face aglow as her muscles tensed, then relaxed around her greedy ministrations. Terry's strokes were short now, the rim of his helmet rarely passing her lips. Although, on the occasions that it did, her lips hungrily devoured the full extent of his shaft. Now there was no doubting the pleasure she was receiving as she gave it; not even when Terry suddenly jolted and gasped, and his seed began bubbling from her mouth, white and viscous amid her saliva.

Still she gave no indication that she ever wanted the moment to end, though his frantic thrusts were pushing the mixture down into her throat. But, as if to make sure she would have no regrets, I stretched alongside her and parted her thighs. They opened wide for me and I raised myself slightly, enough to gaze down at her gorgeous, hairless, gleaming pinkness. Then, lowering my head, I started to eat.

The Ugly Duckling
Primula Bond

The dust they'd kicked up formed a cloud in the cooked air. Odette stretched her neck to relieve the tension. The heat settled on the patches of skin not shaded by her floppy hat and big shirt.

'Let's leave Odious behind!'

How could they not wonder at the undulating landscape, already composed for painting, this humming solitude? A blade of grass, brushed by a careless leg, creaked upright again, protesting. A bleached white stone rolled into a nest of others with a tiny knocking sound.

'You'll get freckles all over your goosebumps!'

'Leave her. Let's get to the shops!'

'*Vaffanculo*,' she muttered in reply. She'd heard the

minibus driver shout something like that earlier. It sounded suitably angry and rude.

Right on cue the honking of his horn shattered the air, shocking a distant church bell into an echo of midday ringing, as if it thought its mother was calling.

There was Miss Drake, draped in her usual flowing turquoise, waving at the driver and chivvying the class. They all glanced up the track where Odette was slowly descending.

'Pit pat paddle pat!' they chanted, waddling into the bus.

The only spare seat was next to Miss Drake. They accelerated with no warning down the hill, spilling Odette's mineral water all over the teacher.

'Careful, Odette! You'll smudge your painting.' Miss Drake mopped at her dress. 'You have an amazing talent, you know. But sometimes I think you're in cuckoo land.'

'Who cares about being the best artist!' Jemima Rivers poked her head over the seat in front while her friend Petra sprayed scent around. 'We only came on this trip to pull some Italian boys.'

'Really, Jemima,' Miss Drake said with a sigh. 'This is educational. We're going to see Botticelli's *Birth of Venus*, and Leonardo da Vinci's *Annunciation*, you know. Florence was the cradle of artistic civilisation –'

Odette stood up to open the window. Bellini's hills and olive groves were flattening into parched verges as the bus charged towards the main road. Jemima hissed into her ear.

'Just keep your head down, Odious, and then Drakie won't notice that the rest of us can't draw for toffee.'

'Talking of cuckoos,' Miss Drake remarked, picking up Odette's sketchbook and turning the pages carefully, 'have you noticed how these girls are blonde English roses, and you're the only dark one?'

'Well, at least I don't burn.' Odette covered her mouth. Her voice sounded too clear now that the braces had been removed.

'No. You have beautiful skin.' Miss Drake spoke quietly, her mouth close to Odette's cheek. 'I know you try to cover up, but I've seen your arms. Like caramel.'

Odette turned, but Miss Drake had leaned back and shut her eyes. Her generous mouth was slightly open as she gasped in the heat. Odette's sunglasses pinched her nose. They were new, too, like her teeth. As she cleaned the lenses she exchanged a glance with Paolo, the minibus driver. His eyes were black, like a bird's, glittering in the sunlight glancing off the passing traffic. Sneering at her ugliness, probably.

* * *

'He's a bit lame,' Jemima remarked later, as they stood in front of Michelangelo's *David*. 'Look at that tiny dick!'

85

Odette blushed. The statue averted his eyes, and stared across the Piazza della Signoria.

'You wouldn't know, Odious,' Petra mocked, fluttering her fingers at her. 'Never seen a real cock, have you? Never felt a big stiff one just for you. Plain eighteen and never been kissed –'

'Well, no bloke could get his tongue past the duck's beak, could he?' Jemima linked arms with Petra. 'I saw some fit guys outside that burger bar. I'm starving, and we've got all afternoon to pull before we have to go back to the villa.'

Odette perched on the edge of the fountain. She had read that Neptune was the guardian of Florence. Why couldn't he guard her from these bullies?

She looked up at David once again. Of course his cock was small. He was about to fight. He was tense. Or would that give him a hard-on? She knew they weren't always like that. Yes, she was a virgin, but she knew they got big and hard. She'd seen the way Paolo's jeans bulged when he arrived early yesterday and saw the others cavorting by the pool. He didn't look at her, swathed in her kaftan. Why would he?

She squinted down at the bright white paper, drawing David's thighs. His groin. The hair curling there. Those muscles running down from his hips, such a different shape to a girl's. She drew the small cock, feeling hot inside as she did so.

You had to sit very still in this heat, not exert yourself except to lift your pencil. The fountain plashed tiny droplets, a shock of coolness before the water melted into her neck and down between her shoulder blades –

'They call it Stendhal syndrome. You look faint.'

The heavy scent of lilies drifted as someone tipped Odette's hat.

'Miss Drake! I thought we had another hour –' Odette blushed and dropped her pencils. 'What's Stendhal syndrome?'

'Named after the French writer Stendhal, who was so dazzled by this city's beauty that he fainted. It happens to people every year.'

'I love it here, Miss Drake.' Odette rearranged her pencils and charcoal back in their tin. 'It's the other girls who make me ill. I thought you weren't coming with us today?'

'I had some business to sort out here in Firenze.' Miss Drake waved her arm round the square and sat down next to Odette. She was wearing pale-pink linen trousers and a billowing chiffon tunic. Her dark auburn hair was in a plait over one pale shoulder. 'I shouldn't say it, but I couldn't bear another five minutes with your mates.'

'They're not my mates.'

'So. Which bit of David do you admire most?' Miss Drake dabbed a speck of sweat off Odette's upper lip with the tip of her finger. 'His manhood? Isn't the eye drawn to that soft beast resting on his leg?'

Odette took her glasses off and frowned at the statue.

'It's too small.'

To her surprise Miss Drake laughed, deep in her throat, the pink gloss making her lips look even plumper. She bit down to stop the giggle.

'I like his hands best,' Odette said after a moment. 'They're a fraction too big, aren't they? And very relaxed, slightly curled, not tensed up for the fight at all.' She smoothed the virgin page of her pad. 'I like men's hands.'

'You have clever eyes, and stunning eyes,' Miss Drake said, peering again under Odette's hat. There was a breeze of lilies again. 'They see how to make the world even more beautiful.'

There was that gooselike honking again and the minibus careered along the side of the Piazza.

'You must have Italian blood.' Miss Drake's fingers made warm dents in her arm. 'I'm meeting someone now. I'll see you back at the villa.'

Jemima and Petra were weaving across the street opposite. A swarm of scooters buzzed around them like hornets.

Miss Drake leaned down, her mouth very close to Odette's cheek. 'See? Even your neck is turning golden now, Odette, where your hat didn't shade it.'

Odette blushed, and started walking back to the bus.

Jemima was slowly bending double. She staggered to the side of the road, no longer laughing, and threw up into the gutter.

* * *

The only sound this early in the morning was the hum of the filter. Every so often the pool's surface shivered, but perhaps it was a thirsty insect.

The villa slouched in sleep, weighted by vines and bougainvillea. Through the kitchen door she could see the cook and maid making breakfast.

There was just time before the lunatics took over the asylum. She never swam with the others. They had laughed so hatefully that first morning at her gangly legs and her overripe breasts squashed into the Speedo swimsuit her mother had tossed into her suitcase. Instead she sat in the shade every day and watched them jiggle about in their brightly coloured bikinis, never actually going in the water, just smearing oil on to each other's sunburn and talking about how far they'd gone with their boyfriends.

No one was up yet. She stretched her arms above her head then dived in. Keeping close to the mosaic floor her body merged and became fluid with the element, her limbs pushing aside the weight of water.

She got out, kissed by the strength of the sun. Just a

few more minutes before they'd all descend, twittering like so many starlings, pecking her out of the way. She sprawled on the hot stones, one leg and one arm dipped into the water. But her sensible swimsuit was irritating her. It stuck to her skin. She arched her back to pull the costume up her hips, taking her arms out of the straps and lowering the front as far down as she dared.

A trickle of moisture started to run down the side of her face. Idly, and with her eyes still shut, Odette ran her fingers over her shoulders, her throat, down over her breasts, pushing under the swimsuit. Her fingers caught on one nipple. It tingled into a tip. She let her hand rest there, the hard nipple trapped between her fingers like a bud. The heat was welding her to the stone underneath her.

A shadow flitted across her closed eyelids. She peered through a fringe of eyelashes.

'*Buon giorno, signorina.*' The black eyes she'd caught in the rear-view mirror were staring at her again, but this time their expression was unmistakeable. A bubble of excitement blocked Odette's throat. From where he was standing he could see her hand stroking inside her swimming costume.

Intoxicated with sunshine, she pulled her hand slowly out. She thought he took a step towards her. But then someone else was coming, floating like a mirage across the singed lawn.

'Odette. There you are! Everything's cancelled!' Miss Drake grasped the back of a sun lounger to get her breath. Against the brilliant blue of the sky she looked white like a spirit. 'You can go home, Paolo,' she said, more imperiously than usual. 'We have no trips today.'

Paolo bowed slightly. '*Come volete.*' He grabbed Miss Drake's white hand as she dismissed him, and bent to kiss it. Odette giggled to herself and let herself drop silently back into the water.

As she floated up she saw that Paolo had gone and Miss Drake was peering at her from the edge. 'What are you doing?'

'Swimming, of course!' Odette pulled herself on to a slab of stone which already glowed tangerine with heat. 'How could I resist that lovely water?'

'They told me you couldn't swim! That's why I came rushing out here.'

'Well, they were talking bullshit as usual.' Odette stretched herself out again. She pulled the straps of her bathing suit off her shoulders. 'Mmm. Is that bacon I can smell?'

Miss Drake laughed that throaty laugh again. 'Nothing wrong with you this morning! The others are all sick as dogs in there.'

'All that beer they drank yesterday.'

'No, no, Odette.' Miss Drake glanced behind her, and suddenly slipped off her robe. She was wearing a kind of

50s starlet-style bathing costume in pale yellow. Her breasts pillowed out of the corseted top, a frilled skirt flared over her pale thighs. She looked like a glorious daffodil. 'This is food poisoning. Good and proper. Salmonella. Dysentery!'

'They don't have dysentery in Tuscany.'

Miss Drake smiled a very wide smile, her red lipstick vivid against her teeth, then swallow-dived into the water. When she came up, right where Odette was dangling her feet in, she almost hooted. 'They'll be out of action for days! So it's just you and me.'

Odette shivered a little, suddenly shy, but then Miss Drake took hold of her wrists and pulled her back into the pool. The water washed over her hot body as the teacher pulled her along the surface of the water then dipped under.

Odette rested on the surface and then Miss Drake sprang up in front of her, hair sleek against her scalp, emphasising her enormous green eyes outlined in what must be waterproof eyeliner.

'This costume is really for posing,' she spluttered, heaving about in the water like an otter. 'The chlorine will ruin it. I'm going to take it off. Can you unzip me?'

She turned and lifted her long plait, and Odette slowly unzipped the yellow bodice so it fell open. Miss Drake didn't move, so Odette unpeeled the costume with some difficulty, down over Miss Drake's ribcage. It was very tight, and sticking to her wet skin. Odette brought her hands round to the front to yank it down and there was the double swell of Miss Drake's breasts. Her heart jumped into her throat and, as she froze, Miss Drake moved slightly, and suddenly the costume slipped right off. As Odette tried to catch it her fingers brushed against the teacher's breasts and even under the water she could feel how big and firm they were. She waited for Miss Drake to screech in horror, but instead her head tipped back slightly, resting on Odette's shoulder.

Odette waited for the teacher to realise what was happening and move away. Her heart was pounding. She hadn't been this close to anyone, ever. She could feel Miss Drake's wet hair pressing on her chin and cheek, but it was the soft bouncing of her flesh against her hands that was twisting Odette's stomach into knots. The other woman's big round breasts were just within her grasp, and she couldn't help it: she wanted to wrap her fingers round them and squeeze. There was another tense pause, then Miss Drake swished forwards so that her breasts were pressed right into Odette's hesitating hands. She wiggled them from side to side for a moment, teasing, so that Odette could feel the prick of the cold nipples. Then suddenly she dodged sideways and flung the bathing suit on to a lounger.

'Now you, honey.' Miss Drake swam back towards Odette, her white skin shimmering almost green like a mermaid. 'Off with it.'

Odette couldn't move. This was her teacher. Her strict but fair teacher who had coaxed award-winning drawings and paintings out of her. Now she was a kind of siren, dark hair and eyes like a witch, fluid body, and that red mouth smiling at her, waterproof lipstick too, and Odette just let her pull her horrible Speedo thing off, her long hands running over Odette's body as she got it over her hips and knees and tossed it aside.

'Lovely, isn't it? *Au naturel.*'

Then Miss Drake leaned forward and kissed Odette. Really kissed her, like the movies, but softer in real life and so sweet. It was electrifying. Her lips rested there, then slid back and forth until Odette's started to buzz, and then Miss Drake pushed harder, pushing her mouth open so that Odette could feel the wetness of Miss Drake's mouth and the tip of her tongue. Odette wanted to suck it, but Miss Drake swam away from her, waited for her, leaning her head against the tiled side, arms outstretched along the edge. Her limbs were feathery as the water shifted, but her breasts bobbed on the surface, firm like juicy fruit.

The knot of excitement tightened in Odette and she swam over, not yet sure what she wanted to do. She glanced up at the house. There was a bit of clattering in the kitchen but the upstairs windows stared blindly back. Miss Drake was looking straight at her, her lips parted, her shoulders out of the water so that her breasts were in full view. Now Odette's nipples hardened up like nuts. She ached to touch Miss Drake's glistening skin. She bounced up against her, her own breasts brushing Miss Drake's arm. Still the teacher watched her, her tongue sliding slowly to the corner of her mouth as if she was finishing a sugary doughnut.

Then she wrapped one arm round Odette and pulled her close. Odette bit her lip, rigid with tension and excitement, the water swaying them gently back and forth. Miss Drake floated her round and on to her back, spreading her arms and legs like a starfish. She could feel no bone, only her own soft, yielding flesh, and then Miss Drake's hands on her breasts, and as soon as she touched them her nipples startled into stiffness again, and then Miss Drake pinched them and excitement shafted down Odette's body so that she arched her back and that made her tits and Miss Drake's fondling hands visible above the water. Miss Drake squeezed harder, floating underneath Odette, and her pussy brushed Odette's bottom, its lips spreading open, the lips rubbing.

'Oh God, Odette, you feel so good.'

Miss Drake pulled her round and they wafted face to face. Miss Drake was staring at Odette's mouth. The wicked expression in her eyes and the moist parting of her lips sent lightning through Odette's belly. She felt drunk with the novelty of it all, the warmth of the water and the flashing of her teacher's eyes. She could feel a smile spreading slowly, her eyelashes fluttering. She was flirting with another woman. Miss Drake smiled back, and wound one leg round her thighs to anchor her.

They were up close now, eyes closed, breasts pressed against each other, and Odette dared herself to brush her lips against Miss Drake's mouth, tickling her lips with the tip of her tongue, and Miss Drake wrapped her arms round Odette and opened her lips in response, her wet tongue pushing in so they could suck on each other and it was super sexy, blowing the top of her head off, she didn't care any more, this felt perfect, now their hips started to jerk and writhe in a kind of dance. Miss Drake hooked both legs round Odette now, she was in charge, she pushed closer and her pussy rubbed on Odette's, and the feeling was so delicious, Odette had touched herself in the dark but this was someone else, someone else's pussy, touching her. Her lips parted to let her tingling clit rub up against her, they danced in a circle to get the full sensation, puss on puss, breast on breast, and now they were kissing really passionately, gasping and moaning at each other.

Under the water Miss Drake took Odette's hand and pushed it towards her pussy, urging her to open it, tickle the petals inside and probe in further, and, as she lay back to let Odette's fingers in, her breasts rose invitingly and Odette leaned over her, nuzzled upwards until her lips brushed the curve of her breasts. She swiped her tongue up and nibbled at one dark, taut nipple. The bud entered her mouth, thrusting up against her teeth, and Odette sucked hard on it, astounded by the wicked excitement that ripped through her. As she sucked there was an answering pull on her fingers, making her bite and suck all the harder. Strong spasms tightened and loosened round her fingertips as Miss Drake started to thrash about in the water, and Odette gave her own little moan of triumph, sucking hard on the tight nipples, ramming her fingers further up Miss Drake's tight cunt while it pulled frantically at her fingers and then her teacher came, unmistakeably, moaning loudly, her head splashing back in the water, body arching in delight, laughing up at the sky.

* * *

Inside the house a clock ticked quietly, a petal dropped on to the terrace, a tiny bird rustled in the vines.

Beside her plate of eggs and warm ciabatta bread was a note.

'I want you to do a self-portrait today, *cara*. We still have work to do. I'll see you later.'

Odette pushed the note aside. Miss Drake had vanished after that amazing scene in the pool, leaving Odette tingling and frustrated. You can all fuck off, she thought. *Vaffanculo*.

She passed the pool, which glittered like crystals, and went into the warm shade of the studio. A huge mirror leaned against one wall. Miss Drake had said it came from a Venetian *palazzo*. The day crept through the crumbling walls, and a finger of light ran down the side of her face. Shadow swathed the rest so that one half of her was suspended in the mirror.

Odette dragged her easel over and sketched before the light strengthened. Her reflection spooked her, without the distortion of her glasses. The emerging eye was almond-shaped, tipping at the corner. She swirled chocolate paint to fill out the iris, then dropped her brushes into a pot of water.

'Do you see the swan emerging as you paint?'

Miss Drake was in the doorway, and despite her sulk Odette's stomach leaped at the sound of her voice. She was wearing see-through mint-green silk.

'I guess.' Odette stared back at the portrait. Miss Drake came up behind her, her reflection flickering in the mirror.

'A tiny present, for a beautiful swan.'

In a bag was a fuschia bikini. Odette laughed. 'Thank you, Miss –'

'Call me Aurora. Just while we're alone.'

And there it was again, that warm mouth on hers as Miss Drake knelt in front of her and kissed her slowly, her tongue pushing in for Odette to suck on it while Miss Drake's hands easily pulled off the old shirt and shorts to find the bare skin beneath, and this time it was Odette who lay back on the old couch in the shadowy corner of the studio while the heat blazed outside, while her teacher ran her hands over her brown body and teased it into arches of desire, sucking on her nipples, kissing her way down her belly, stroking, always stroking, and finally parting her to lick at her pussy, long swiping strokes with her tongue, brand-new sensations, a woman's tongue, her art teacher's tongue, licking her most private parts, nibbling her clit, pushing her tongue into her like a soft wet cock and caressing the rest of her until she felt those waves of ecstasy pulsing through her, strong enough to drown, and she bucked and moaned under Miss Drake's tongue as she came.

* * *

Much later, when she was snoozing by the pool, counting the seconds until Miss Drake gave her her next lesson, the others stumbled from the villa like the undead.

'My God, Odious! You look, like, amazing in that bikini.'

'Miss Drake gave it to me,' she said smugly.

'Teacher's pet!'

Petra slapped Jemima's pale arm. 'Button it, Puddleduck.'

Jemima scowled. 'Where are your glasses, Odious? What's going on?'

Odette leaned right over the water. They all crowded round to stare at her reflection and they could see, as the water stilled, the brown eyes slanted like a swan's, the sleek hair, the tanned skin and perfect teeth.

'Yes, she's my pet, my sexy, beautiful pet, and I don't care who knows it.' Miss Drake was suddenly standing at the poolside, hands on hips, her sleek legs planted firmly apart. 'Now go and pack, you little bitches.'

Then she leaned down to stroke Odette's face, kissing her hungrily as she did so.

'I have to pack, too,' said Odette, her whole body yearning against Miss Drake's.

'No, you don't. You and I are staying here. For the whole summer. And then you're going to my new academy, right here in Florence.'

And as they kissed, pulling off scraps of silk and bikini, Odette could swear she saw faces at the windows of the villa, green with envy.

The Game
Kyoko Church

When I first met Bill I didn't understand that he was hitting on me. He was quite a bit older, after all. I really did think that he was just very passionate about books, liked to discuss them. It didn't occur to me at the time that a university professor would have no lack of colleagues and students with whom to discuss the latest author in the *Quill & Quire*. Why would he need to come every week into the public library to do that with a lowly library clerk? Call me naïve.

Eventually we did go out for coffee and I began to get the picture. If you had told me a month before that I would be seeing a forty-something-year-old man with grey at his temples and a hint of crow's feet beginning to appear around his eyes, I would have called you a liar, but, well, there you have it. And just how he managed to open me up, to take me from a relatively introverted yet independent 23-year-old to someone willing to spill all her most intimate, private secrets and willingly relinquish her power, I couldn't tell you. But he did.

I remember the first time he asked me how often I masturbated. There we were, sitting in Starbucks looking for all the world like perhaps a daughter discussing course selection with her father. Maybe a car loan. In fact, Bill smiled wide and asked me how many times a day I brought myself to orgasm manually. Like he was asking after my health. Like you might ask someone how often she drinks water or brushes her teeth.

The weird thing was that it didn't seem weird. He could do that. Make the extraordinarily intimate seem everyday. It was in my mind for a couple of moments to lie, to feign surprise or even disgust at the suggestion that I would engage in such an activity, let alone on a daily basis. I was about to. But something in his face made the words stick, stop at my mouth. I stammered a bit and finally admitted that it was something I did at least twice a day; usually in the morning, sleepily, still half in my dreams, and then again at night, in order to fall asleep.

His response was enigmatic. At the time.

He took a sip of his coffee and swallowed slowly, smiled again, then *tsk-tsk*ed his disapproval. 'That,' he said softly, 'will never do.' Which was in complete contra-diction to what that smile said. What that smile said was, That *will* do. That will do very nicely.

Had I understood at the time it would have been prophetic.

During this conversation he was the picture of calm authority. It was this Svengali-like aura that led me to divulge such private leanings. Later, though, he told me how his heart was racing in anticipation of my response, how desperate he was to know if he had guessed correctly, if he had accurately read all the signs indicating that I would be such a perfect playmate. Signs? I asked. He gave me another of his enigmatic smiles in response. I can't describe it, he said, almost to himself. It's something in the way you walk, in how you move, how readily you laugh. It's how you tilt your head, the tone in your voice. I could tell.

* * *

So that's how this whole crazy thing got started between Bill and Jake and me. Oh, I haven't told you about Jake yet, have I? I guess I'm getting ahead of myself.

You see, I didn't understand what this was between Bill and me. We weren't really dating, all we did was have coffee. And then, of course, our chats. But I'll get to that.

So when Jake came up to me at the bar one night, offered to buy me a drink and started chatting, I didn't discourage him. Plus, did I mention he's gorgeous? Jake is like Josh Duhamel and Colin Farrell's love-child. I know, it's weird. But boy, does it work. All biceps and brawn. Mm. That first night I rubbed up against him on the dancefloor like I was a cat and he was the scratching post. And speaking of pussy, by the end of the night mine was dripping. So I barely protested when we were making out at the back of the bar by the ATM and Jake shoved his hand down the front of my jeans. His fingers slipped into my sopping hole and were instantly bathed in my slippery wetness. I felt Jake's hard-on, which was pressed against my thigh, pulse harder and he muttered in my ear, 'Baby, you are my kinda girl.' He slicked his fingers up and down my clit in a steady rhythm that had me coming in no time, gasping and riding out the waves on his hand. 'God, you're like on a hair-trigger!' Jake exclaimed.

To be fair, I wasn't always so eager.

* * *

It started after my coffee-shop confession. That night Bill texted me before bed.

'Why don't you be a good girl tonight. For a change. You may play with your naughty little pussy. But don't come. I'll be by tomorrow. To check.'

That one text did it. Something in me responded to that. My heart leapt. My pussy throbbed. I felt it through my entire body. I didn't understand why but that one little text got me hotter than any porn I'd ever seen or smut I'd ever read. 'Be a good girl. Don't come.'

I followed his instructions and he did, as promised, come by the next day. To check. In his car, in the library parking lot on my break, he slid his hand up my thigh, under my skirt, into my panties. He fingered me slowly, briefly, and smiled. 'You didn't come,' he said. 'Well done.' I don't know how he knew. He probably didn't. He was probably faking. I was pretty sure he was faking.

'Are you a good girl?' he whispered, looking in my eyes, his fingers still inside me.

I didn't know how to respond. What answer was the right one? What did he want?

'Yes.'

'Good,' he said, taking his fingers from my moistening pussy and starting to rub my clit.

'Mmm …'

'You like that?'

'Yesss,' I murmured.

He rubbed a little harder, a little faster. 'I want you to show me what a good girl you are.'

'OK,' I said, eyes closed, feeling the tension from my night without release building in my body.

'You let me play with your pussy, rub your clit, just

like this,' he said as he got a rhythm going and my hips started moving. 'Mm, yes, that's good.' He rubbed faster still. 'And just as it's feeling really good –' he rubbed and my hips bucked '– just as you're starting to come,' he said, rubbing really fast and hard while I moaned out my pleasure, 'then I stop.' He pulled his hand away.

'Ah!' I gasped and my eyes flew open. 'Fuck!' I grabbed at his hand to try and pull it back to me but he only chuckled.

'I thought you said you were a good girl?' He smiled. He stared into my eyes like he was looking for something. 'You are even more beautiful,' he sighed, licking his fingers, 'when you're desperate.' He leaned over then and kissed me for the first time.

* * *

Our chats were every night before bed. Sometimes in the morning too. He would message me or call me and tell me what to do, how to touch myself. Fast, slow. Hard, soft. He'd have me tease myself to the edge, get so close. Stop. Again. Stop. Five, sometimes ten times. There was one rule. Don't come.

I was so horny. I was horny all the time. I woke up horny. I went to bed horny. My days were a blur of inane conversations and daydreaming about fucking. My nights were a collage of wet, nasty, humping dreams. And yet

106

Bill and I still didn't fuck. I begged him. But no. He said for now he was teaching me how to be a good girl. How to have control over my body and not give in to its silly whims.

Then Jake put his hand down my pants at the bar that night and it was all over. Or rather, something new began.

* * *

I don't know exactly what I expected Bill's reaction would be to the fact that I was seeing Jake. Hurt, maybe. Jealous. Angry. Or possibly just annoyed. But when I finally told him that Jake and I had been out a couple of times I was expecting some kind of negative emotion.

What I got, however, was far from it.

'How old did you say he was?' We were at Starbucks again, with our grande coffees.

'He's a year older than I am.'

'Did you fuck him?' Which makes it sound like he was angry, but that's not how he asked it. He asked in the same tone as his first question, about Jake's age. Like you would expect a child to sound, asking about a new possible playmate who's moved into the neighbourhood. Interested. Intrigued.

'Would you be upset if I had?'

'Only if you came,' he said.

Remembering that first night at the bar, I looked at Bill and swallowed.

'I see,' he said, stern now.

'No, we didn't have sex but he, I,' I stammered. 'I couldn't help it! He was touching me and you'd been teasing me ...'

'Shhhh,' Bill said. 'Have you come since?'

'No,' I said.

'Why not?'

'Because you told me not to,' I said, like an admonished little girl. 'I didn't want to disappoint you,' I whispered.

'Ah.' He smiled widely. 'That's my good girl.' He stroked my hair. 'Well, what's done is done. All that matters now is how we deal with it.'

'Deal with it?' I asked.

'Of course,' he said. 'There have to be consequences. I mean, I'm glad you're still trying.' Then, in barely a whisper, he added, 'But you have to be punished for being such a come-hungry little slut.' Under the table he cupped my mound in his hand, his middle finger pressing down against the slit. 'For having such a greedy little pussy.' I felt my insides flip, my sex pulse.

He stood then, grabbed my hand and led me out of the café. We went to his place where he spent the next five hours administering his punishment. I realized our teasing chats were nothing. Nothing compared to completely giving over control. Touching myself was one thing. But being tied down to his bed, legs spread, helpless, while he had total access to my sensitive flesh was another. He stroked, tongued, buzzed, reduced me to a quivering mass of flesh begging, begging to be released. And each time I got close, each time he saw my legs quiver, my clit throb, heard my screams reach a certain pitch, he'd stop. 'Are you going to let that boy make you come again without my permission? Are you going to fuck him behind my back?'

'No, Bill,' I gasped.

He began stroking again, still ignoring my pleas. 'You may not come,' he commanded. 'You may not.'

When did I realize that Bill was also into guys?

Well, I wouldn't even say that Bill was 'into' guys. Bill was into sexuality. He was into people. He liked situations. Power play. The sex of the players was just another compelling factor.

Jake was much less complex. I was a girl he liked and, I guess like most 24-year-olds, he just wanted to get in my pants. Or more into them than he got that first time. And that wasn't happening.

I didn't intend to start teasing Jake. But you can see how it turned out that way. Since Bill was keeping me ramped up without release, I had to let my frustrations out somehow.

That Friday, at my apartment, Jake went to take my jeans off and I stopped him. He pleaded again, as he had done since that night at the bar, 'Come on. You know you want to.' He kissed my neck and whispered, 'Let's fuck. It'll be so good.' How could I explain? Bill won't let me. I'm saving it. For what?

When I finally had Jake's enormous cock in my mouth, my saliva running down his shaft while I pumped it with my hand, and I heard him start to groan, 'Oh fuck, that's good. Oh yeah, baby, I'm close,' I couldn't help myself. I slowed down.

The frustrated cry he let out was music to my ears. 'Oh fuck, go faster. Please. Please!' he begged and his begging made my pussy moisten. When he put his hand on the back of my head, well, I had to tie him up then, didn't I?

Bill wanted to know all about it. About Jake. And I told him. I told him that, although he seemed a little embarrassed by it, he liked it when I played with his nipples. That when I put the restraints on him his cock got harder. That when I flicked my tongue on that sweet spot, the frenulum, where his cock head meets his shaft, he went crazy. That he didn't like me going near his asshole but when I rubbed the spot behind his balls he nearly lost it.

Bill listened. Intently. He took it all in. I could practically hear his brain whirring as he filed it all away. For what? At what point did I know it would come to this?

* * *

'What the fuck?' Jake was not impressed. 'You gotta be fucking kidding me.'

We were at Bill's house. I told Jake I wanted him to meet a friend of mine. I led him to believe there would finally be sex. Perhaps I used the word 'threesome'.

This was not what Jake had in mind.

'I'm not doing any fucking homo bullshit. If that's what you're thinking.'

Bill smiled. 'Gay, straight,' he said. 'They're just labels. I'm sure I could have you coming in five minutes, my friend.'

Jake looked stunned.

'Listen,' Bill said, as he placed three glasses of wine on the coffee table in front of where we sat in his living room. 'I think we're both here because we're interested in the young lady.' He winked at me and motioned me over. 'You see, I've been trying to teach her some patience.' I sat beside him as he began fondling my breasts. 'You've no doubt noticed she's quite … eager?'

Even Jake couldn't hide a smile at that point. He watched as Bill pulled off my top and began pinching my nipples through my bra and I could see he was conflicted but he was also getting turned on in spite of himself.

'She tells me you haven't fucked yet,' Bill said conversationally, unclasping my bra.

'Oh, what, so you guys are fucking and that's why she won't be with me? This is fucked up, man,' Jake said. But he didn't get up.

'Quite the contrary. Despite her begging I've managed to keep this little slut from jumping on my cock.' Bill's hands roamed all over my body now. 'She won't fuck you because I won't let her.' I was getting wet from his manual attention as well as his words. Jake also appeared to be enjoying the show. Jock that he was, he was wearing track pants that did nothing to hide the effect the sight of me half-naked and horny was having on him.

'But alas, even I am only flesh and blood. I find myself growing impatient to have her tight little cunt,' he said as he pulled off my dampened G-string panties from under my skirt, giving Jake a full view of my shaved pussy. 'So it appears we both want the same thing.' He stopped touching me then, grabbed his wine and sat back. He took a sip and said, 'Care to make it interesting? Say, with a little game?'

What Bill managed to get Jake to agree to was just another indication of the power of his persuasiveness. I hadn't been sure what he had in mind when he had asked me to bring Jake over. Horny as I was, I was pretty game for anything.

'Five minutes,' Bill was saying. 'All you have to do is

last five minutes. If you do, you get to fuck her and I'll watch. If you don't, then I'll be the one to fuck her.'

'Dude, you're not sucking my dick,' Jake said. 'No guy is going to put his mouth on my cock. I'm only here 'cause she's so fucking hot. I told you, I'm not into guys.'

'Well, this is going to be so easy for you then, isn't it?' Bill pulled over a chair from his kitchen. 'Tell you what, you sit here and I'll just use my hand. Just my hand,' he said, putting it up in an innocent gesture as if to say, 'It's a hand. We all have them'. 'I won't even use lube,' he said, chuckling, adding, 'in case that's "too gay" for you.'

'You think I'm going to come in five minutes from being stroked with no lube? By a dude? Ha!' Jake looked at me, still just wearing my skirt, like he was putting his eye on the prize. He came over, grabbed me up and kissed me long and hard, putting his hand up my skirt and sticking a finger in my pussy. 'Mm, I can't wait to get my cock inside here, baby. If the old man wants to watch, I got no fucking problem with that.'

Jake hadn't agreed to the restraints. Or the blindfold. But he could come up with no good reasons to argue. After all, the blindfold just meant he couldn't see Bill so what was the problem?

Of course I knew. Bill had played a similar game with me during my hours of punishment. I knew what it was like not being able to see the clock. To have no idea how much time had elapsed, how much longer you needed to hold out. And Bill knew what the restraints did to Jake.

And he knew a lot more. Thanks to me.

With Jake on the chair naked, bound and blindfolded, Bill came over to me and gave me a kiss. 'Enjoying yourself?' he whispered as he caressed my breasts. His hands were warm and dry. I imagined how they would feel to Jake.

I was enjoying myself. Immensely.

* * *

Not that I'm any hand-job expert, but I had never seen a guy being jerked off like that.

When Bill started Jake was already semi-erect, presumably from watching and touching me, thinking about what we were about to do. In five minutes. According to Jake.

Bill was seated beside Jake in another chair. Using just his forefinger on the underside of the shaft and his thumb on top, Bill very softly and not very quickly stroked upwards only, over and over, just at the top of Jake's cock, right under the head. Right where I told him Jake loved it. After a minute he was fully erect.

Then he took two fingers and rubbed the pads of them

up and down that spot, still lightly but rapidly. Jake moaned. Bill went back to the slower thumb-and-fore-finger technique. Then he used all of his fingers to lightly rub over the head, in a gentle unscrewing motion. Grasping Jake's dick, he used his thumb and rubbed circles all around that sweet spot. Then back to the quick up-and-down technique.

At the two-minute mark Jake started panting a bit. Up until this point all of Bill's stroking was very light and all concentrated on that sensitive spot. But when Jake started to pant Bill encircled his cock with his whole fist and gave it a few firm up-and-down tugs.

'Ah! Fuck!' Jake exclaimed. Bill went back to the rapid-fire strokes with his two fingers. 'Oh God,' Jake said, his legs starting to shake. 'How much time left?' Not even three minutes had elapsed.

'Seems our little slut isn't the only eager one,' Bill quipped. But on hearing Bill's voice Jake seemed to gain a little control back. His legs stopped shaking. His cock, however, remained hard.

It appeared Jake was doing battle against his will. His cock strained for firmer sensation as Bill rapidly teased his sensitive frenulum. Yet Jake was trying to hold back. After another thirty seconds, his legs started to shake again. 'Fuck!' he panted, as Bill, still rapidly strumming that spot, encircled his cock head with his thumb and forefinger. Jake moaned. Then Bill took the palm of his hand and rubbed it more firmly all the way up and down Jake's entire shaft. 'Oh God!' Jake cried. It was the sensation his cock was straining for. 'Fuck! How much more time?' I glanced at the clock. Four minutes, twenty seconds. But Jake didn't know that. Bill continued rubbing with his palm like he was petting a beloved animal. 'Ohhh!' Jake moaned. I could see he was holding back with everything he had. 'Fuck me.' He put his head back against the chair as Bill went back to the rapid jerking under the head. 'Ohhh! Fuck! It's a dude, it's a dude, it's a dude,' he moaned to himself. Four minutes, forty seconds. He can make it, I thought. Only twenty seconds left.

Then Bill reached down with his other hand, reached under Jake's balls and pressed that spot. The other spot I told him Jake loved. Continuing with his rapid-fire strokes on his cock, Bill massaged Jake's prostate. Jake held out a few more seconds but it was no use. As Bill grasped his clamouring staff firmly in his fist and jerked him hard, still massaging, Jake let out a strangled scream. The alarm went off just as the first spurt of come shot out of him, the force of the spasm propelling it across the coffee table, on to my leg.

* * *

In the end it was the best possible outcome. For me.

Fair's fair and it was a tie. I would just have to fuck them both.

At the same time.

Bill did let me come. A lot. The whole session seemed to have a celebratory air, after all. I don't know that I could have held back if he hadn't, anyway. After watching what Bill did to Jake I was so worked up I could hardly stand. But that was OK. There wasn't a lot of standing involved.

Bill didn't let me off that easily, though. We moved to his bedroom and, as Jake jacked his own shaft this time, impressively getting it to rise again despite his recent explosion, Bill set about strapping me down again firmly on to his bed. 'Now,' he said, testing the straps, ensuring my immobility, 'you need to explain to Jake just what a horny slut you are. In case he hasn't figured it out already.' I gulped in embarrassment, despite everything. 'Tell him all about what you've told me, how you can't keep your fingers out of your pussy.' As I spoke Bill stroked my clit, fingered my hole. When my voice quavered, if I gasped from his ministrations, got distracted, he'd chide me. 'What's the matter, slut? Are you so horny you can't even string a sentence together? See, Jake,' he said, holding up his glistening fingers, a shiny, thick thread of girl-juice strung between them. 'A wet, horny, cock-crazy slut.'

Jake's member had risen to all of its previous glory at

this new exhibition. 'Say it,' Bill said. 'Tell Jake what a horny slut you are, how much your pussy craves to be filled, and I'll let you have his cock. But you have to say it.'

I said it.

I would have said anything.

It felt like it was for ever that I had been imagining what it would be like to have Jake's thick member inside me. So when he eased it into my sopping, shaking pussy while I lay tied and helpless across Bill's bed, all I could do was moan in sheer ecstasy at this feeling of fullness, finally, after so long without. My sex quivered around his bulk. Then Bill, kneeling beside my head, silenced me with his thinner cock in my mouth. They both slowly pumped in and out. All I could think was: more. More.

Bill leaned over then, spread my labia and began tonguing my clit. My aching pussy stretched full with a massive pole, my sensitive clit teased by a lapping tongue, I could hold back no longer. Cock and tongue wrenched that orgasm out of me. I gasped and choked as I simultaneously felt my mouth and pussy fill with come.

* * *

After an evening of fucking two men that I had lusted after for so long, fucking them in every way imaginable and coming more times than I can honestly remember, I can't say I learned what Bill was trying to teach me about patience. But Jake learned something. About not being such a homophobe. About labels just being labels.

Slut was another label too, Bill said, as he reminded me that, even with his permission, there would be consequences, and compensation extracted for my evening with Jake and him.

Would I ever learn my lesson? he asked. I didn't know.

But I would certainly have fun trying.

You Already Know
Charlotte Stein

I tell him not to, I tell him, 'Get the fuck out of here,' but he doesn't. Of course he doesn't. He's as big as a bull, as big as a brick wall, and he just bulldozes right into the store and takes Mickey D around the neck as though he's nothing, and throws him over the counter.

Of course, everyone knows Mickey D is no good. He shirks his responsibilities, as Mr Kirkpatrick would say – but that doesn't mean he has to be thrown over the counter. It doesn't make it right and fair that this bull has him crying and bleeding on the floor of Mr Kirkpatrick's store, for something he owes or something he has or has not done.

Even I know that. I'm pathetic, and I'm weak, and I

don't know anything about drugs or whatever this guy is into, but I understand that much.

'Stop,' I tell the bull, and he turns and looks at me with his mad, blazing eyes.

Only they're not mad and blazing at all. He looks wounded, I think, like someone stuck him in his side. The matador waved his cape and he charged, and now there's a lance through his body. Soon he's going to bleed out on the floor of this little grocery store, and no one will care because he's the guy who threw Mickey D over the counter.

He's the guy who works for some drug lord or thief or pimp, and nobody cares about guys like that.

Least of all me. I just stare at him and stare at him, until he steps back from the counter. Mickey D is crying somewhere behind it, snottily, but the bull pays no attention. He just looks at me until I notice other weird little details about him.

His eyes are the colour of melted chocolate. He has a tattoo on his arm – a big Star of David. The grain on his shaved head is the colour of a million little iron filings, so rich and real I can almost imagine them sifting through my fingers.

Even though there's nothing to sift.

And then he backs off, and walks right out the door.

* * *

121

Next time I see him, he's not beating the shit out of anybody. But the stench of a million battles hangs all over him, like a soldier returning from a war he didn't want to fight. He's leaning against the truck he drives around in, shoulders too tense for someone who's meant to be looking casual, cigarette dangling from one hand, unsmoked.

He flicks it away when he sees me coming down to open up. It's 6 a.m.; the light is the same colour as that grain on his head. On his face now, too, because he hasn't shaved and there are deep shadows around his too-curved jaw.

There's something in his face, I think. A roundedness all over that cuts against the sharp masculinity he wears everywhere else. It's in his eyes, too – those eyes that aren't like chocolate at all. They're deep and fathomless and when he calls out, 'Hold on there a second,' they tell me a thousand things he doesn't want to say.

I'm just not sure what all of them are.

'Hold on there,' he says, and I think about Mickey D flying through the air. I think about him panting, full of rage or aggression or something else altogether, and I want to run. I want to tell him, 'Get the fuck out of here,' just like I did in the store.

But I don't.

'Your friend,' he says, then pauses as though he's waiting for me to recall who he's talking about. He licks his bottom lip, and I notice it's very fat and full, and also chapped. 'He did some bad shit, got it?'

I don't know what to think. It's like an explanation, only not. It's like an explanation he needs to punch into my gut, though I'm surprised as anyone to find I'm still standing when he's done. I go one worse than that, in fact.

I blurt out: 'Is that all you've got to say for yourself?'

And I don't even know how or why. It just comes out of me, as jagged as I thought he was, and when I'm done he stares at me like I've gone mad. Maybe I have. He could punch me for real right now and I'd go down so hard, so hard. Hell, he wouldn't even have to punch me. He could just swipe me with the back of his hand and I'd be bloody and sore tomorrow.

But he does none of those things. Instead he runs a hand over the bristle on his head, and when he does I see his knuckles are as raw as fuck. They're not just bloody – they're split and scraped and there's a glimmer of something shiny in amongst everything, as though somehow he's gone right down to the bone without gushing everywhere.

He doesn't even seem to notice, however. He just seems … tired.

'What do you want from me?' he asks, only it comes out all run together in that gravelly voice of his. It's like he's entirely made up of building materials: rocks and iron filings and the stuff you line driveways with.

'I want you to come inside,' I say. 'So I can take care of that hand.'

* * *

I don't know why I say it. I suppose it's because I can't get it out of my head, once I've seen it. It looks disgusting, and it's even worse under the queasy fluorescent lights of the store's bathroom.

'What did you do? Punch out a wall?' I ask him, but he doesn't answer.

He does something better than answering. He cocks one eyebrow at me, and the corner of his mouth turns up – almost like he's smiling, really. Yeah, almost.

'You know, if you look like a thug and act like a thug, people are going to think you're a thug,' I tell him, but again he doesn't say anything. He just lets me run his knuckles under some warm water, a hiss or two coming out of him every once in a while. I watch the little sink turn red, then white again, and then finally there's nothing but a series of tiny pink mouths along the heavy bumps of his knuckles.

And me holding his hand, as though it's something separate from him.

'Stay there while I get something to put on it,' I tell

him but really it's only so I can go out into the store and catch my breath. Stop the shakes I've fallen into, somewhere in between touching his hand and right now.

However, when I go back in there I'm still doing it. And I think he notices, too, because his eyes go all over me in little stuttering fits and starts, and as I paint Bactine over his knuckles he asks if I think he's going to hurt me.

'No,' I say, but I don't know if I'm telling the truth.

'I'm a thug though, right?' he says. 'Maybe that's all I'm good for.'

I put strips of white over the little mouths, to hold them closed – neatly, I think. Fussily.

'I don't think so,' I say and he replies:

''S that why you're being good to me?'

Though I hadn't really thought it was the case. His knuckles just looked rough, that's all, and I wanted to see to them. It was me – the urge to make them all right again, to do what he hadn't, to do what he probably never does.

And then he says: 'Maybe you just want me to be good in return, huh?' in this new kind of voice – this curling, deep-down sort of voice – and I can't respond. I know what he means, of course I do, but I can't tell him to back off or get out or any of the things I know I should go with.

They won't come to me, no matter how hard I pull.

'You want me to be good to you, baby?' he asks, and maybe it's that word. The one on the end, the one that isn't my name. Or maybe it's the way he puts a hand on me – so much gentler than everything else about him would suggest.

He just rests it on my hip, as though he could take it off any second. All I have to do is say the word and he'll go away, he'll never have existed, he didn't come into the store the other day and throw Mickey D over the counter.

Only I know he did and I can feel that hand, those long thick fingers, stroking the material of my little grocery-store uniform into fine little wrinkles. He doesn't bunch, or tug, or rip. It's just those little wrinkles like he's ruffling feathers.

'I'll be so good to you,' he says, and I believe him, I do. I don't know where it comes from or why it's in me now, but I believe him enough to let him lean down slowly, and press his mouth to mine.

He's soft on the upper lip and rough on the lower, just like I'd thought. But there are other things I don't expect, like the strange half-smoke, half-cinnamon taste of him, as though he chews Big Red between each cigarette.

And his hands go up instead of down, circling over my back until I'm boneless and wondering what it's like to be the kind of girl who fucks someone in a

126

grocery-store bathroom. Is that the kind of girl he usually has? Up against some tiled wall somewhere, clothes barely off? Mouths hard and clashing, almost too rough to stand it?

Only then he says: 'You live upstairs, right?'

And I don't tell him no. Apparently I'm the kind of girl who takes strange, bullish guys up to her apartment when she's supposed to be opening up her place of work, and when this guy says lie down on the bed and spread your legs, she does it.

I do it.

I spread my legs over my flower print coverlet, and he just comes right on over and slides his hands up my thighs. Underneath my dress, underneath all of my clothes with everything about him strange and too big in my neat little bedroom, one of his massive knees making my mattress dip and his face set to that almost-smile he sent me before.

His eyes glitter in the half-light and I can't speak, I can't breathe, he's moving too slow and I thought this would be fast. Like someone ripping a Band-Aid off, quick and painless. You don't even have to look.

But I do have to look, because he's right there and now his hands are at my panties. They twist the elastic into spirals, and tug so slow it's almost maddening.

'This what you want?' he asks, but his flickering smile says he already knows. My breath is coming in weird little hitches, and once he gets my panties around my knees – almost off, but not quite – the scent of my arousal hits the air.

Of course it does. I'm as wet as a river. He hasn't even done anything and I'm so slick it's embarrassing, my body like a wire strung too taut – but worse than this is the fact that he can tell it. Before he puts a single finger between my legs he can tell, and I think the idea makes him hard.

I can certainly see something, pressing against the rough material of his pants. And when he shifts on the bed the view gets better, until I'm sure I can make out the exact solid curve of his stiff cock.

Is it weird if the sight makes me wetter? I suppose the weird thing is how wet I was before anything really sexual happened, but I can't think about that now. I don't want to think about anything but his hands on the insides of my thighs, and then, after a moment, his body between my spread legs.

'Wider,' he says, and I obey. There's nothing else for it, really. I might as well just do whatever it is he wants, and then I can simply slide back into the way my life was before, as though nothing ever happened. Service was not interrupted.

I did not let him put his face between my legs, I swear to God.

Only I did, and I know I did because when it happens

I'm so shocked I put a hand over my eyes. I make a little noise, thinking of all the things I expected him to do. Get his cock out and fuck it into me bareback, ride me hard then leave me wet and wanting on the bed. Maybe something dirtier – something I can't even think of and don't really want to – and then him laughing afterward.

But instead he cups my thighs with those big rough hands, and dips right down as graceful as a cat. Like maybe he's going to bite me somewhere, but decides to kiss at the very last second. Right when I'm on edge and I'm staring into the blackness behind my hand, sure it's going to be one thing then getting another.

Of course I think of skinny Brad and the boy I had before him – the one who bought me flowers and seemed like a real swell guy. I think about the way they pressed their mouths to mine, all teeth and sloppy wetness, nothing smooth or sweet or calm.

And then I think of this bull between my legs, with the iron filings coating his scalp – the ones I can feel burring beneath my fingertips when I dare to just reach down and touch him – and his hands like shovels. The brutish swell of a million muscles working beneath every item of clothing he wears.

The Star of David blazing on his massive bicep.

And I forget about flowers and skinny Brad and everything I've ever believed in. His mouth is like silk. He doesn't lick: he *strokes* me with his tongue. He doesn't suck: he *draws* me into him.

He makes a million romance clichés between my thighs, and when I arch my back he does them all over again, in spirals.

Feels like he does it for hours, though realistically I suppose it's only been a few minutes. All of this teasing, all of him pressing down on my thighs until I'm good and open for him, all of this flickering over the very tip of my clit … it's just a little bit of time, really.

So why am I bunching the sheets up into my fists?

I try to tell myself not to. He'll know it so bad, if I react the way I want to. He'll get that I'm so close to coming – so close it feels like agony – and then he'll smile his little half-smile and I'll be trapped for ever.

I fight it. I keep my mouth pressed tight closed and when he sinks a finger into me like he's just testing the waters, I bite down hard on my lower lip. Not enough to make it bleed but close, and oh, it feels good to get that bit of pain.

It's what I need to keep me above the pleasure swelling through my clit. He's barely doing anything at all to it, really – every circle he makes around that little bead feels as though he's studiously avoiding it – but somehow that's worse.

It's building and building, and it's going to be terrible when it finally comes. And I think he knows it, too, because the more I struggle against it the tighter he winds things, using two fingers instead of one, pumping harder and faster in response to the sounds I make, his free hand almost like a restraint on my thigh.

Though I'm sure I could get away if I wanted to. Positive. Any second now I'm going to get up, and walk right out the door. Go downstairs to the store and continue my life as it was. Any second now.

And then he swipes one long stroke right over the tip of my clit and, oh God, I come, and come, and come.

* * *

Next time he comes by, Mickey D cowers. Mr Kirkpatrick says: 'You'd better get out of here, you!'

But I don't do any of these things. I just stand there with the broom still in my hand, and think about him kissing between my legs the way most men have never even kissed my mouth. I think of the spiral patterns on my ceiling, and how for the first time in my life I didn't notice them during sex.

Though I guess technically he didn't have sex with me. It was just a *kind* of sex – maybe just foreplay, when I really think about it – and then he had simply stood and walked back out of my bedroom.

Though I lie when I say that. He hadn't simply stood and walked out. He had looked at me as he backed towards the door, this expression on his face like ... I don't know.

Like maybe I surprised him, and the surprise amused him greatly.

Which I suppose I should be mad about. I mean, I'm not something to be amused over, you know? I'm a decent person and I do the right thing when called on and I'm not a sex maniac, or anything.

So why am I looking at his big, rough face while thinking, Do it again?

This time, he takes my dress off. I don't say he can, and I don't ask him to. He just turns me until I'm bent over the bed, and unbuttons everything back there. Undoes my apron and lets it drop to one side. Spreads everything once he's done so I'm only clothed over the front of my body, but bare at the back.

It's a weird feeling. Like being separated from myself – I'm separated from myself and then he rumbles that he's going to do the same thing he did the day before. 'You OK with that, you OK?' he asks, but I can't answer.

I think I'm shaking. I think there are tears running down my face but it's fine – he can't see me. He doesn't need to know what I'm doing as he sinks to his knees and licks and licks over my swollen sex.

Though I'm pretty sure he can tell when I come within a minute, and sob too loudly for anything inside me to take, and then, oh, then he runs a gentling hand down over the curve of my back.

It's too much. Be rough, I think at him, but he isn't like skinny Brad. He's not like the swell guy with the flowers. He says, 'Easy baby,' and then he *asks* me. He *asks* me:

'You OK with me taking you, now?'

And I can't say anything to that. If I open my mouth I might beg.

But he gets to me before I have to endure a thing like that. He turns me back over and spreads me across the bed, most of his own clothes still on. Most of mine gone. And though I don't want it to happen with my face wet and all of me mixed up like this his mouth finds mine.

His big arm goes around me.

I'm not even sure when he starts fucking me – though the word *fucking* is stretching it a bit. It's stretching it a lot, in fact, because he rocks me slow and easy and there's something unbearable about that. So much so that a hot rush of anger goes through me, unaccountably, and the urge to bite him or dig my nails into his back swells up.

The urge to tell him, 'Do it hard' comes up with it, but it's difficult to say words like those with a soft mouth on yours, and everything like a long, smooth roll into bliss, and his big arms around me – God, his arms right around me.

It's like he's holding me as I go down.

And, even better than that, I can *feel* him moaning. I can feel him doing it all the way through my body, because his mouth doesn't veer from mine and his voice is like the distant rumble of thunder.

Mine sounds faint, by comparison. Faint, but I hope he can hear and feel it anyway. I hope he knows I'm clinging to him, instead of digging my nails in. I hope he knows how good this is – how each stroke of his thick cock strikes me just right, pushes me a little bit further into bliss.

But then he pulls away just long enough to gasp, 'You gonna come, baby?' So, in all honesty, I think he knows. He can probably feel it, bubbling up through me. He should *definitely* be able to feel my pussy clenching around his ever-working cock, and, even if he can't, the words I get out do the rest of the job.

'Oh God, oh God, I'm coming,' I gasp.

But I only say God because it occurs to me in that moment of bliss – I don't even know his name.

* * *

It's early morning, and that sweet bluish light is just starting to creep under the drapes. I watch it make its way over all the ordinary things in my apartment, and then finally it gets to him and paints the solid curves of his gorgeous arms. It slants shadows over the side of his face, the heavy slab of his cheekbone, the delicious curve of his perfect mouth.

I don't know when he started sleeping over. Probably some time after I dared open my mouth to ask him what his name was, right in the middle of a hot and sweaty fuck session. He had grinned, at that – not offended the way I expected – then said: 'It's Tyler, Bethany.'

Oh, I wish, I wish, I wish I'd told him things had to end, then. I should have let things go the moment I realised he already knew my name, but I think it was too late even then. It was too late when he stared at me with those wounded eyes. It was too late when he leant against his truck, cigarette in hand.

It's too late before it's begun, with Tyler.

He stirs and turns over and my heart stirs with him. I'm lost, God, I'm lost.

'You OK, kid?' he asks, before he's even opened his eyes. Maybe he can tell I've got my back pressed too tight to the headboard. Maybe he can tell I've been gazing and gazing at him like some lovesick puppy.

Lord, when did this happen? When?

'Man, it's early,' he tells me – just for something to say, I guess. But then he follows it with this, right out of the blue: 'Love you, kid.'

And that isn't just something to say. I don't know where he gets these things from, I really don't. I don't know how he's this person inside – it's impossible, it's awful, I can't look at him.

'You love me, right?'

He sounds so sure, and I'm glad. Mainly because I can't speak and even if I managed to I'm sure I'd do something dumb when I did. Blubber, probably. Laugh it off, this thing we've got – this thing born out of fists and brutality and bitter lives made up of nothing.

It's good that he keeps talking, really – right past everything I can't say.

'How come you never answer?' he wants to know. 'I ask you a question, you never answer. Afraid the answer's yes, huh? Don't wanna get caught out saying yes to the likes of me.'

He's smiling, though, when I look at him. The teasing smile that tells me I don't have to really say – and then I realise. It floods through me, the understanding of how he is different to every other man I've been with.

'I never have to answer with you,' I say, and I think of those big arms of his holding me as I fall down, down, into this sea of strange love. 'You already know.'

Making Up Is Hard to Do
Terri Pray

'You can't trust him, Annie. You heard that slut; he's been meeting her twice a week.' Janet pushed the empty glass to the edge of the table and waved at the waitress. 'Going back to him would be a mistake.'

'I just don't know. OK, everything she said makes sense. It fits with his schedule, but when I looked him in the eye and confronted him – you didn't see the look in his eyes, Jan. He was hurt. I mean really hurt.' Her stomach knotted, settled and then knotted again. Had she done the right thing in walking out on him? Dave was a good man, at least she'd thought so until all of this had landed in her lap.

'Just because you've been with that jerk for over a year, doesn't mean that you owe him the right to walk over you.'

'No, but I owe him the chance to tell me his side of the story, don't I? I mean, he'd do the same for me.' This wasn't like her. She didn't act like this; she was the type who got to the bottom of the story before she made a decision.

Except this time she hadn't.

'I have to go.' Annie waved at the waitress, trying to get her attention.

'No, Annie, wait. You can't just go back to him. He's won if you do that.' Janet reached across the table, taking hold of Annie's arm. 'Stop and think. If you back down on this then he owns you. For the rest of your life he'll own you.'

Annie took a deep breath and pulled free. 'No, he won't. I'll just be giving him the same consideration I'd give someone else. I know better than to take one side of a story as the truth. That – that woman is trouble. She's always been trouble. I've watched her deliberately break up other relationships and she's had her eyes on Dave for a long time.'

'Annie …'

'No, I've got to do the right thing here, Jan. I have to get to the bottom of this.' She looked up and sighed in relief as the waitress set the bill on the table. 'Thank you.' She pulled a twenty from her purse and handed it over before she turned her attention back to Janet. 'I'll let you know what happens, just hope he's willing to listen to me.'

'Annie please …'

'You're wasting your breath there, Jan. Let me deal with things my own way, please.' She stepped around the table and hugged her oldest friend. 'I can't risk walking away from him without at least trying to get to the bottom of this.'

'I can't help but think that you're making a mistake.'

* * *

Janet's words played through her mind as she slipped behind the wheel and pulled out of her parking spot.

'She's wrong. She has to be wrong,' Annie muttered, glancing in her rear-view mirror. 'Focus, girl! Concentrate on driving.' Easy to say, harder to do. More than once her attention drifted from the road and by the time she pulled into the driveway her hands were shaking.

Only one light was on in the small house they shared and that light flickered, shifting from moment to moment. The house she'd walked out of three days ago because of that damn fight.

Was he alone?

What would she do if he wasn't alone?

Her throat tightened. If he wasn't alone she'd grab a few things and leave. Then get the paperwork started to get him out of the house. After all, it was her wages that paid for the lease, and the lease was in her name, not his. Would she even need paperwork?

No, she couldn't think that way.

Her hands shook as she pulled the key from her bag and slid it into the lock, listening.

Nothing. No sound. Not even the TV or radio.

Was he even home? Maybe she should have called first? She knew better than to simply walk into a place unannounced, but this was her home so maybe the rules didn't apply.

'Dave?' She reached for the light, fumbling to find it.

A hand closed over her mouth, a firm grasp pulled her against a strong chest, a familiar voice now a harsh whisper against her ear. 'You were expecting someone else?'

Despite everything she struggled. She knew who it was. She knew his scent, the feel of his body, the way his hands felt on her body, yet she tried to break free.

'Was there something you wanted to tell me? Or are you ready to listen to me now?' He loosened his grip enough to let her speak.

'I came back to talk this out.'

'Ah, but not listen?' His hard cock pressed against the curve of her buttocks.

'No, I ...'

His hand closed over his lips, a gentle pressure but enough to silence her. 'I didn't cheat on you. The only woman I want is you.'

Her heart raced, nipples hardening, pressing against her bra.

'You're the only woman who leaves me so hard that it hurts.'

A soft roll played through her hips as a moist warmth dampened her panties. She tried to speak but the light pressure across her lips urged her to remain silent.

'I didn't go out with that slut. I didn't kiss her. I didn't so much as hug her. It's you I want. You I crave. And you that I'm going to have, unless you want to kick me out of our home? All you have to do is tell me to go when I move my hand, and I'll leave. If you don't trust me, then there's no point in staying together. Even though it will kill me to leave, I'll walk out and never bother you again.' He slowly moved his hand away from her mouth. 'All you have to do is tell me to leave.'

Her throat tightened. Did she believe him? Did she dare take that risk of losing him?

She closed her eyes, replaying his words. He loved her. He trusted her. He wanted her. All of that confirmed that she should have known better than to doubt him. He'd never given her reason to do so prior to that bitch sticking her nose into their business.

Her hips rocked softly back against him, teasing the hard outline of his cock. God, how she wanted that within her.

'Don't go,' she pleaded. 'I'm sorry; I should have stayed and listened to you the first time.'

'Then trust me. Trust me enough to not hurt you, not

unless you want that touch of pain. Trust me enough to love you and guide you. Do you trust me, Annie?' He nibbled her left ear, his teeth grazing softly over the curve and down to the lobe before he sucked it into his mouth, flicking it with his tongue.

She groaned, her eyes half closing as she leaned back against him. 'Yes, I trust you.'

'Good.' He let go of her ear. 'Then let me show you how much you mean to me.' He reached down, taking hold of her left hand, releasing his grip on the rest of her body.

Annie nodded, squeezing his hand in return. 'All right.'

Dave led her through to the living room until they stood in front of the only source of light in the room, the fireplace. She glanced around, but a sharp tug on her hand brought her focus back to him.

Where it should be.

'Last chance to back out, Annie.' He brushed one hand through her hair, loosening the thick dark braid until her hair tumbled over her shoulders.

'I'm not going to change my mind.'

'Good. Now, close your eyes.'

She hesitated a moment, then obeyed. Her nipples ached beneath her clothing, heat rippling through her core. What did he have in mind?

'Don't open them.'

'I won't.' She smiled despite the tremor of fear that

shivered a path down her spine. Fear that curled its way into her belly and down between her thighs, coating her nether lips with a warm, intimate cream.

'If you do, I'll have to spank you.'

Oh God, this was so damned wrong. The idea of being spanked by him was actually turning her on. That had never happened before. She didn't get off on that type of thing.

'You're trembling,' he growled against her ear.

'Yes.'

'Maybe I should find out how you react to a stronger hand, hmm?' He tangled one hand in her hair, using it to guide her across the room, closer to the fire, or so it seemed from the increase in warmth. 'But first, you're wearing too much.' He was behind her, his hands cupping her breasts, his thumbs teasing across her hardened nipples.

'Maybe you should help me with that?' she whispered.

'No, I think not.' He stepped away from her, leaving her with her eyes shut and alone. 'Strip for me.'

'How, when I can't see what I'm doing?' This was insane. She'd fall, or hurt herself or something like that.

'You don't need to see in order to know how to remove your clothing, Annie.' His words sent a thrill of pleasure through her.

She reached for the buttons on her blouse. She couldn't

see, but he was right, she could still do this. 'Why do you want me to do this?'

'Trust. It's all about trust.'

She had to try and learn to trust him again. No, it wasn't about that, it was – was about showing that she did trust him. The words weren't enough.

She opened the first button, her heart racing, nipples aching. How long would it be before he touched her again? Her fingers trembled as she opened the second button. Was he watching her? Yes, of course he would be. Why else would he have her do this?

Her inner walls fluttered, desire building as she imagined him watching her every move. Was he hard? She flushed at the thought.

'Slowly, I want to enjoy every moment of this,' he cautioned.

Annie smiled and ran the tip of her tongue over her lips. His voice was husky. She'd heard that huskiness before when he wanted her.

'What will you do when I'm undressed?'

'Patience, Annie love. Patience.'

Easier said than done.

The buttons opened one by one under her trembling touch, and she slowly pulled her blouse out of her skirt. She took a deep breath and eased it back down her shoulders before she let it fall to the floor. 'Did you want me to remove the skirt?'

'No, your bra next.'

She reached behind her back, finding the hook-and-eye set-up of her bra. It took her a moment to unhook the bra.

'Keep your hands behind your back, Annie.'

She tensed, but obeyed him, her breath hitching in the back of her throat. Her arms strained as she held position, her back arched, breasts lifted but still contained within the confines of her bra. 'Why?'

'I like the way you look like this.' Something touched her left nipple. A brief caress that tore a soft moan of delight from her lips. 'Helpless. Offering everything you are to me.'

A soft roll moved through her hips as he brushed something against her right nipple. Her mind screamed at her to move, open her eyes, do something, yet she struggled to hold position. 'Y–you've never done anything like this to me before.'

'And you're complaining about me doing it now?'

Annie shook her head.

'Then what?' he growled against her ear.

Annie struggled to find the words even as her body's response to him, to everything he was doing or might do to her, threatened to consume her ability to speak.

'Tell me.'

'I – I want this.'

'Yes?' He cupped one breast, squeezing lightly.

'I want more than this.' The admission cost her.

'Why?' He moved his hand, closing a finger and thumb on her nipple.

'I was wrong,' she breathed.

'And ...'

God, could she say this? Her inner walls clenched, weeping with the need to feel his cock deep within her body.

'Answer me.' His fingers closed, a jolt of pain lancing through from her nipple down to her clit. Her hips jerked, pressing, seeking him out.

'Dave, I – I was wrong.' That was enough, wasn't it?

'Continue.' His voice brooked no disobedience.

'And when someone is wrong they – they need to be punished.'

'Hmmm, and how do you think you should be punished, my Annie?'

Her heart raced against the walls of her chest. Was it her place to suggest something? She opened her mouth to speak and then stopped.

'Well?'

Her throat tightened, but she struggled to speak. 'I don't think – think it's my place to say how I should or should not be punished, Dave.'

'Sir.' The word was a heated breath that caressed the side of her neck.

She bit back a groan at the word.

'Say it.'

'I don't think it's my place to say how I should be punished, sir.' Her cheeks burned as she obeyed him.

'Very good.' There was a moment's pause where he moved away from her. The lack of his touch left her aching and uncertain. 'Keep your eyes closed.' His hand was back, brushing against her cheek before he moved to touch her hair.

She shivered, then arched, crying out in shock as his fingers tangled and tightened in her hair.

'Don't fight me.' He tugged on her hair, bringing her head down to waist height.

'Sir, please ...' she pleaded.

'Just relax and trust me.'

God, how she wanted to but it wasn't easy. With her hands behind her back, her balance was off. She spread her legs a little more, trying to find her centre of gravity, a soft whimper slipping from her lips.

Dave gave her a moment, and then used the grip on her hair to lead her across the room. She fought against her instinct to open her eyes, or move her hands, desperate to prove to him that she could do it. She'd never seen this side of him before and didn't want to do anything that would prevent him from sharing it with her again.

'Good, very good. Now, put your hands down.'

She frowned but obeyed him. Her fingers found something fabric-covered and it didn't take her long to realise that it had to be the couch. The arm of it now rested against her belly. She sighed in relief and pressed her hands against the cushions, relieved to know that she was no longer solely reliant on her own balance or the hand in her hair.

Dave reached under her skirt, shoving the material up about her waist. A moment later he gripped her panties. Without warning he yanked them down, leaving them halfway down her thighs.

'Much better, don't you agree, my Annie?'

'Yes, sir.' She swallowed hard, forcing her mouth to work. Her belly knotted in shame. There she was, with her panties down around her thighs waiting for what?

His hand connected with her bare buttocks with a loud crack that lifted Annie on to her toes. She cried out, her head jerking up, her eyes snapping open.

'Y–you spanked me!'

'Yes.' He smoothed the offending hand over her stinging backside. 'Close your eyes, my Annie. You don't want to displease me again, do you?'

Her heart sank. 'No, sir.' She closed her eyes and tried to relax. She deserved to be punished. She could accept that. It had been her idea to be punished for what she'd done to him.

'You. Should. Have. Trusted. Me.' Each word punctuated by a swift smack against her upturned ass.

Annie writhed over the arm of the hair, sobbing as

she struggled to hold position. Her fingers dug into the cushions of the couch. Her breath hitched in between the sobs, mascara now a runny mess down her cheeks and still he continued.

'I. Have. Never. Betrayed. You.' The blows came faster now, each one lifting her on to her toes. He barely gave her time to think between the spanks and yet she couldn't find it within her to tell him to stop.

'I. Love. You!' The last three were the hardest of all and yet they stopped her tears.

Her buttocks burned and the heat clawed its way down her thighs and up between her legs. Liquid desire coated her nether lips and she whimpered, lifting her heels and offering her backside to him once more.

'What is it, my Annie?'

'I need you to …'

'To what?'

Could she say it?

'Annie?' He cupped both ass cheeks in his hands. 'Tell me. Tell me what you want me to do.'

'Fuck me.' The words came out in a soft, pleading whisper.

'Ask me, Annie.'

'Fuck me, sir. Please.' She ran the tip of her tongue over her lips. 'I need to feel you inside me. I – I have to make it all right but I need to know that you want me still.'

149

'Oh, there's no doubt that I want you. I've never stopped wanting you. Even when you were yelling at me, accusing me of cheating on you, I wanted you.' He shifted behind her, the sound of his fly opening filling her ears. 'And I'm going to show you how much I still want you, Annie.'

The head of his cock pressed between her thighs and she wanted to scream in joy. This man. This wonderful man, who had stood there, letting her accuse him of all the wrongdoings in the world, still loved her. Loved her and wanted her despite her faults.

'Beg me to fuck you.' He leaned forward, tangling his fingers in her hair. 'I want to hear you beg.'

Her back arched, hands clawing at the couch. She'd already asked, why did she need to beg?

To make it all right between them. So there was no doubt that she wanted this. No question in the minds of either of them.

'Sir, I'm begging you to fuck me. I need you. Please. Please sir, fuck me. Fuck me till I scream. Till I pass out. Please.'

He growled behind her, and thrust into her warm, wet and oh so very willing pussy.

Annie arched beneath him, pressing her body back against him as his cock filled and stretched her slick core. 'Yes,' she sobbed in delight.

'Is this what you want?' He pulled back, one hand in

her hair, the other on her hip. 'Is this really what you want, Annie?' He slammed back into her, his balls slapping against her nether lips.

With her panties still around her thighs she couldn't part her legs very far. Between that and the way he held her over the arm of the couch, her body remained taut, her inner walls tight and rippling along the length of his cock.

'Is it?'

'Oh God, yes!'

A sharp slap connected with her still heated backside. 'You forgot a word.'

'Yes, sir. Yes, sir, this is what I want!' She tried to turn her head, wanting to open her eyes. Wanting to see his face. But the way he held her, his fingers so tight in her hair, prevented Annie from turning to look at him.

'Over the arm of the couch. Knickers around your thighs. A red spanked bottom. Is this really how you like it, my Annie?'

'Yes, sir. Yes. Always and for ever.' She rolled her hips, pressing back to meet each thrust. Her skirts tangled around her waist, her nails digging into the fabric. The inner walls of her slick pussy clenched around his cock. Each time he pulled back she arched up to meet him again.

Wanton. Willing. Wet.

'You're mine, Annie. You'll always be mine.' He tugged back on her hair a little more.

'Yes, always yours, sir.' Let it be so. Please just let it be so.

'Open your eyes.' He let go of her hair and pulled out of her pussy, leaving it clenching, bereft of his cock.

She whimpered and opened her eyes, finding her balance once more over the edge of the couch. For a moment her vision swam.

'I'm giving you a choice, the last one you get this evening, Annie. You can either go to the bedroom where I'll make slow, sweet love to you. Or we can finish here. But if we do it here, it will be hard, merciless, and you'll get no choice in what I do to you. Your choice, Annie, here or the bedroom?'

There was a part of her, a small part, that wanted the long, slow, tenderness of the bedroom. But the way her body ached, the heat that seeped round from her well-spanked backside and into her throbbing, untouched clit …

'Here,' Annie whispered. 'I want it here, sir.'

He grasped her by the hips, one hand pushing down against her back, forcing her face against the cushions. She'd barely realised what was happening before he parted her thighs until they strained against the material of her knickers, and set the head of his cock against the slick lips of her pussy.

She tensed, trying to brace herself. It didn't help. He slammed into her body, his fingers digging into her hips even as his other hand kept her body arched over the arm of the couch. She cried out, head jerking up, ass lifted from the thrust.

Each new thrust was harder than the one before, knocking the wind from her, stretching her inner walls. She sobbed, trying to meet him. Pressure, pleasure, pain, they all combined within her body. Humiliation, oh God, she'd never felt like this before, so ashamed yet wanton. Desperate to move, yet wanting so much more. Willing to give up control and wanting it to be taken at the same time.

'You're forgiven, Annie. Do you understand that? I forgive you.'

'Yes, sir,' she cried out, lifting to meet his thrusts. 'Thank you, sir.' Forgiven. It was over. He wasn't upset with her any more.

'You. Are. Mine.' He growled, lifting her up so her feet no longer touched the floor. She was helpless like this. No way to ease the thrusts. Nothing that would protect her from the force of what he was doing to her.

And God, she liked it!

Each new thrust sent a wave of pleasure through her body. The pressure grew but all she could do was help-lessly accept what he was doing.

He'd moved the hand from her back so he gripped both of her hips, yet her knickers still prevented her from parting her thighs very wide. The tension added to the friction and his thrusts forced her against the cushions, her hair caught across her lips, tangling there, but none of it mattered any more. Only the way he filled her, his balls slapping against her slick nether lips with each harsh thrust. Her breathing became ragged, her body no longer her own, as she tried to react, to lift, to move with him, but all she could do was submit to him.

'Dave, please!' She couldn't hold on any longer. The pressure was too much.

'Say it properly, Annie. Don't let me down now.'

'Sir, please, I have to come! Please, let me come!' She squirmed beneath him.

He growled in delight, his fingers digging into her hips. 'Come for me, Annie. Come for me now!' He thrust one last time into her slick core, his breathing as heavy as hers.

Her body took over. Her inner walls spasmed around his cock, heat and need rolling into one as she arched and pressed back against him. Her mind reeled even as her body surrendered to him in one long shuddering, gasping, sob of release.

For a moment she didn't move. She couldn't move, her legs shook and didn't want to work, and her mind was unable to grasp the idea of standing up.

He eased his cock from her body and wrapped his arms about her waist. Slowly, taking care that she didn't fall, he lifted her back up on to her feet, then turned her to face him. His dark eyes filled with a glow she'd never seen before as he cupped her chin in one hand.

She opened her mouth, trying to speak, but his lips claimed hers, his tongue parting them, delving into her, tasting, touching, claiming, taking what little breath she had left. Her knees, already weak and unsteady from what they had shared, threatened to give out on her, but he kept his arms wrapped about her, supporting her as he broke the kiss.

'Mine.'

'Yours,' she agreed, unable to say anything else.

'No more fights.'

She shook her head. 'No – no more fights.'

Dave scooped her up into his arms, nestling her head against his chest and wordlessly carried her towards the bedroom.

Annie smiled, and did the only thing that made sense. She surrendered.

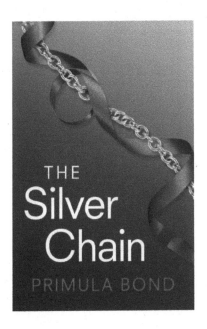

THE SILVER CHAIN – PRIMULA BOND

Good things come to those who wait…

After a chance meeting one evening, mysterious entrepreneur Gustav Levi and photographer Serena Folkes agree to a very special contract.

Gustav will launch Serena's photographic career at his gallery, but only if Serena agrees to become his companion.

To mark their agreement, Gustav gives Serena a bracelet and silver chain which binds them physically and symbolically. A sign that Serena is under Gustav's power.

As their passionate relationship intensifies, the silver chain pulls them closer together. But will Gustav's past tear them apart?

A passionate, unforgettable erotic romance for fans of *50 Shades of Grey* and Sylvia Day's *Crossfire Trilogy*.

GAME – JUSTINE ELYOT

The stakes are high, the game is on.

In this sequel to Justine Elyot's bestselling *On Demand*, Sophie discovers a whole new world of daring sexual exploits.

Sophie's sexual tastes have always been a bit on the wild side – something her boyfriend Lloyd has always loved about her.

But Sophie gives Lloyd every part of her body except her heart. To win all of her, Lloyd challenges Sophie to live out her secret fantasies.

As the game intensifies, she experiments with all kinds of kinks and fetishes in a bid to understand what she really wants. But Lloyd feature in her final decision? Or will the ultimate risk he takes drive her away from him?

Find out more at www.mischiefbooks.com

POWER PLAY – CHARLOTTE STEIN

Now she's the boss, everything that once seemed forbidden is possible…

Meet Eleanor Harding, a woman who loves to be in control and who puts Anastasia Steele in the shade.

When Eleanor is promoted, she loses two very important things: the heated relationship she had with her boss, and control over her own desires.

She finds herself suddenly craving something very different – and office junior, Ben, seems like just the sort of man to fulfil her needs. He's willing to show her all of the things she's been missing – namely, what it's like to be the one in charge.

Now all Eleanor has to do is decide…is Ben calling the kinky shots, or is she?

Find out more at www.mischiefbooks.com

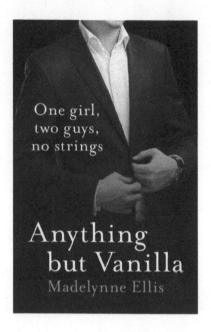

ANYTHING BUT VANILLA
MADELYNNE ELLIS

One girl, two guys, no strings.

Kara North is on the run. Fleeing from her controlling fiancé and a wedding she never wanted, she accepts the chance offer of refuge on Liddell Island, where she soon catches the eye of the island's owner, erotic photographer Ric Liddell.

But pleasure comes in more than one flavour when Zachary Blackwater, the charming ice-cream vendor also takes an interest, and wants more than just a tumble in the surf.

When Kara learns that the two men have been unlikely lovers for years, she becomes obsessed with the idea of a threesome.

Soon Kara is wondering how she ever considered committing herself to just one man.

Find out more at www.mischiefbooks.com